# IN THE TEETH OF IT

*A Gingerbread Hag Mystery*

*- Book Two*

By K. A. Miltimore

*To all the readers who have supported this series and provided their valuable feedback and support. Thank you so much.*

 ISBN: 9781075196256



Cover Illustration by Edison Crux

Other works by K.A. Miltimore:
The Gingerbread Hag Series - Books 1 - 3;
Pink Moon Rising - The Witches of Enumclaw;
The Necromancer and the Chinchilla - Short Stories from the Gingerbread Hag

# CHAPTER ONE

Two months and not a sign of Lyssa. For two months, they had watched and waited and worried, but despite the fox's warning that something was watching them from the dark, nothing had happened. Life doesn't stand still, even when there is a threat from an ancient demigoddess.

The guests of The Gingerbread Hag moved on with their lives. Bren Aldebrand, the visiting salamander, decided to continue on to New York, still unsure whether he would renounce his life if he had the chance. Anahita Sohrab, the undine, decided to change her plans as well. She was not going on to Alaska, but instead staying in Seattle; Mel would join her once she started college in the spring.

Hedy too had made a decision; she had decided to reopen the waystation for travelers.

Despite her worries that maybe they had not really seen the end of Lyssa, she knew that her role as a host of a waystation was too important and too much of her own identity to give it up. She contacted the Concierge and let them know that the waystation in Enumclaw was back in order. Being a waystation host was who she was - without it, Hedy knew she would feel adrift and alone.

The bakery was busier than ever. The small article in The Courier-Herald had been picked up online and had drawn in more business; customers were now making their way there from Tacoma and Seattle. Hedy found that she couldn't keep up with the demand on her own so when Mel offered to help until she left for college, Hedy had hired her on the spot. Not only had Mel proven herself reliable and someone that Hedy really liked, but she already knew all the members of the menagerie and their peculiar ability to speak. Hedy couldn't have asked for a better assistant.

The front door bell tinkled and the rain blew in with the open front door. Mel hustled to shut it behind the customer. She was in the entry, focused on decking the halls with all of Hedy's Christmas decorations, and it was a huge job. Hedy had boxes of decorations and the entry was already overcrowded with her huge collection of strange curios and knick-knacks; Mel struggled to make the entry look festive and not a cluttered mess. She wished Anahita was there to lend a hand, but they only saw each other on the weekends, and it was only Wednesday.

She missed Ana. They had only known each other for two months but she couldn't imagine her life without the elemental. Springtime and moving in together in Seattle couldn't come soon enough.

"Dreadful weather, ugh. I could hardly see the road driving into town there was so much water. Good thing I had your address in my GPS because your sign is really small." The customer gave her umbrella a slight shake over the mat on the floor and then put it into the available stand.

"I'm glad you made it safely. I hear it is supposed to dry out some later in the week. Welcome to The Gingerbread Hag. How can I help you?"

Hedy, as always, wore her criss-cross apron and had her white hair done up in a lofty beehive style with tiny Krampus pins tucked in here and there. Krampus featured heavily in the shop during the holidays, given Hedy's roots in the Black Forest.

"I have an ugly sweater party to attend tonight and I want some unusual treats to bring with me. I read about your shop online and thought I would come check it out. I came up from Tacoma." The woman shed her slicker and she was indeed sporting a very ugly Christmas sweater underneath. Hedy, herself no follower of current fashion, really didn't understand the whole ugly sweater thing. But to each their own.

"Well, I have some of our usual items, such as the foxtail donuts or our rat sugar cookies, which are always popular. But for the holidays, I have some Krampus cupcakes and I have our cannibal gingerbread men cookies." She waited as the woman examined the showcase and watched her expression turn from curious to astonished to excited.

"Oh yes, the gingerbread men are perfect. I love how you've baked them to be eating gingerbread limbs. How perfectly awful! I'm not familiar with Krampus, but he looks very devilish indeed. I should take a few of those as well."

"Krampus is an ancient legend from Germany. He predates Santa Claus, in fact. You can think of him as an opposite version of Santa. Instead of bringing treats for good kids, he whips and abducts bad children. He's been scaring kids to be good for centuries." Hedy had the large box carefully packed with the cannibal cookies, and another smaller box with six Krampus cakes. The customer took both boxes and handed back her credit card.

"Your shop was definitely worth the drive. Are you on Instagram? I'd love to follow you."

Hedy couldn't count the number of people who had asked her this question in recent weeks. She'd have to ask Mel about it and whether she should try to get online; Hedy didn't even own a computer.

"I'm afraid I am rather old fashioned, so no Instagram for me. Have a wonderful time at your party tonight." Hedy said, handing the card back to the customer, along with her receipt. Mel held the door open for the woman as she retrieved her umbrella and faced the whipping wet wind.

"How are the decorations coming?" Hedy joined Mel in the entry and saw that things were definitely still in progress. To be fair to Mel, Hedy knew it was a job that would take considerable time, given all the decorations.

"Well, I think I have the garland all up. The banister is done, and I added it above the doorways. I can't for the life of me figure out that wooden pyramid thingy though, and I'm usually the one who builds the Ikea furniture at my house."

Mel's reference was lost on Hedy but she wasn't surprised that the pyramid had been a struggle. It was an eight-sided platform with several tiers and it looked far more complicated than it really was.

"I'll show you how it goes together. It is a *Weihnachtspyramide.* Think of it like a multiple layer carousel that spins from the heat of the candles. It's a staple in Germany, but not as popular here, I'm afraid." Hedy had many years of practice assembling the pyramid and she had it together quickly, building it in the center of the same large table that she used for tending to Ren, the injured fox, back in October. Hedy wondered briefly how the little fox was doing.

"Look at all those little figures. These all look like scenes from a fairytale, with a woodcutter and forest creatures. What is that devil looking thing, though?" Mel took a closer look at the tiny wooden figure that looked like a devil with a very long red tongue. She hadn't been in the shop that morning when Hedy made her first batch of cupcakes.

"Don't tell me you don't know about Krampus either? Good grief, I thought the Internet had brought everything to every corner of the world. Apparently, there are still some secrets out there."

Hedy retold her short description of Krampus to Mel, who promptly pulled out her phone and Googled for more information.

"This is seriously a thing? Men dressing up in fur suits, wearing wooden masks, and ringing cowbells to scare away the ghosts of winter? Sounds goofy to me." Mel was pulling plaid bows out of a box to tie to the garland.

"Well, goofy or not, it's an old tradition and this is the time of the year for celebrating tradition, right? Where do your people come from? What are your traditions?" Hedy had finished assembling the Christmas pyramid and was lighting all the candles to demonstrate how it worked.

"My grandma on my dad's side said we were from Scotland. My mom's family is Native American - Salish tribe. My family really doesn't do much when it comes to tradition. I mean, we celebrate the holidays and visit family, but nothing like old Krampus here."

Mel handed the little wooden figure back to Hedy, who placed him in the pyramid, near a group of rowdy children.

"I don't think it matters how big or small your traditions might be. It's just nice to mark the year and remember where you've been. Tradition can be as simple or as elaborate as you like. Personally, I like things elaborate. I'm sure that doesn't surprise you." Hedy emphasized this by pulling a rather large straw goat out of a box. When Mel looked bewildered, Hedy said simply, "The Swedish yule goat, of course."

"Of course, how silly of me." Mel would have a lot to tell Anahita when she met her this weekend. "Oh, I forgot to tell you," Mel continued, "did you see that new shop that opened in town this week?"

Hedy shook her head; she had been so busy baking that she had barely had a chance to run out for groceries.

"It's called 'the Red Bat,' I think. It opened up in the building next to where the yoga studio caught fire. Looks like it would be right up your alley."

"Why is that, Mel?" Hedy wasn't exactly sure what "up your alley" might mean in this context.

"Old clothes - sorry, vintage clothes, and accessories. It's a small shop but it looks jammed packed with things that fit your style." Mel gave a crooked smile and continued tying bows. Hedy's style was eclectic, to say the least.

"Hmm, I wouldn't think a small town like this would be a great location for such a shop. But then, here I am with this bakery." Hedy laughed and drew a small log out of the box, with the face of an old woman carved into it. The front door bell tinkled as Darro filled the doorway.

"Not fit for man nor beast out there. I have your tree, Miss Hedy. It's sopping wet so I have it drying here on the porch." Darro was barely visible under his black slicker hood.

"Oh, let me see it." Hedy hurriedly followed Darro back to the porch and stood on the sheltered side to inspect the blue spruce that was dripping water everywhere. It was enormous, probably close to eight feet tall, and full of fresh needles.

"It's lovely, Darro. Where did you get it?" The gardener was shaking his slicker to get some of the rain off it and managing to splatter Hedy in the process.

"That tree farm out near Mount Enumclaw. They have the best trees. It cost an arm and a leg, but you said spare no expense, so here 'tis." Darro followed her inside and peeled off the slicker, which Hedy gathered up before it could puddle on the floor.

"Come in and let's settle up for the tree. Plus I want to hire you to hang lights outside." She hung the slicker on the coat rack with the mat underneath. With the rain they had been having, it was necessary to keep the water off the hardwood floor.

"Aye, I can do that. What's this? I haven't seen one of these since I left Scotland." Darro picked up the small log and ran a thumb over the carved face.

"What is it?" Mel had finished her bows and came over to the table for a closer look.

"See the face there, carved in the wood? In Scotland, if you burn a *Cailleach*, a log with the face of an old woman carved in it, you'll take away the bad luck for the year. My gran burned one every year. They don't always work, though. Gran could have told you all about that." Darro set the small log back down on the table, and his expression looked very far away.

"Darro, come into the shop. I have some shortbread I'd like you to try; I tried a new recipe and I need an opinion. Mel, you are welcome to join us. We can't really finish in the hall until the tree dries out anyway." Hedy led the way back into the shop, where Darro took a seat and Mel went behind the counter to roll out pie dough.

"Any news from our man, Bren? He's been gone about a fortnight," Darro asked, taking the shortbread and a cup of tea with a grateful nod.

"Nothing as of yet. He promised to send word when he reaches New York, so I suspect he is still on his way." Hedy wanted to believe that, but it didn't take two weeks to travel to New York by train. She couldn't bring herself to admit that maybe Bren had forgotten all about them - forgotten all about her. The thought was too painful to speak aloud.

"And Miss Ana is doing well? Living in Seattle, is she?" Darro directed his questions toward Mel.

"Yes, she found an apartment near the University and we see each other on the weekends. I've even convinced her to get a cell phone, which is a big step forward." Mel chuckled and shook her head in wonder; how anyone could function without a phone was beyond her.

"That's good to hear. And no sign of the other

then?" Darro didn't have to say her name; they all knew who he was talking about.

"Not hide nor hair. We've been watching for weeks but nothing has come to pass, thank goodness. Maybe she didn't survive the wound in her side."

Hedy still thought about the feeling of sliding the knife into Lyssa almost every day. No matter how hard she tried not to.

"We should be so lucky. With Jeffries dead and his house torn down, perhaps that is all behind us." Darro didn't wish to speak ill of the dead, but the fact that Mr. Jeffries hadn't survived his burns from the fire didn't trouble him a bit. The man was a monster.

"Yes, let's hope so." It had been two months of worry and watching for all of them. Hedy felt the weight of it draped on her, like a heavy coat she couldn't take off.

"A new year and much to look forward to. I'd be very glad if all that is truly behind us," Mel chimed in, her thoughts still on Ana and warmer, spring days.

Hedy wanted to believe it could all be over but something in her gut told her that things were not finished, no matter how it seemed.

"Oh, Mel, I forgot to tell you that I received a call from the Concierge today and we will be having a new traveler coming, likely tonight or early tomorrow. Whatever time you can spare to work in the shop would be much appreciated, especially since we have the big Christmas market coming up this weekend." Hedy pulled the candied fruit filling for the pies that Mel was making from the refrigerator, placing it near the fluted pie tins.

"Sure, I was planning to be around this weekend anyway. My family is going to the tree farm tomorrow and then we'll all be going to the Christmas market at the fairgrounds on Saturday. Ana will be here." Mel said, feeling that bubble of anticipation rising in her belly at the thought of her girlfriend.

A girlfriend, a beautiful and magical girlfriend. A girlfriend who would be meeting her uncle and cousin for the first time. The realization of family introductions put a slow pop to the bubble. She didn't know how that would go.

"Wonderful. I haven't seen her since early November so be sure she stops by my booth to say hello, won't you? And if she needs some money, I could use her help in the shop too." Ana wasn't quite as skilled as Mel, but Hedy could definitely use her eager assistance.

"Oh, Ana is quite set for money, but I bet she would be willing to come help out while she is in town. You know Ana."

"I best be on my way, Miss Hedy. The tree was one hundred and eighty dollars, if you don't mind. I'll string up the house lights on the first dry day for a flat hundred, not including the lights." Hedy exchanged his empty shortbread plate for three hundred-dollar bills.

"I have the lights, Darro. Beautiful white and pale pink glass bulbs. I hope you aren't afraid of heights, because I want them all along the peaks of the house."

"I'll have them on every dormer and cranny, don't you worry. If the weather is right, it will be tomorrow. Thank ye kindly for the shortbread. It wasn't up to Granny's standard, but it was good enough for American tastes." He chuckled as he rose and found his slicker in the hall. With a wave of his hand, he was back out in the wet wind.

"I don't think I will ever make something up to his granny's standards. I've been trying for two months now." Hedy chuckled but it actually pricked at her pride. She prided herself on being an excellent baker and the fact that she couldn't master something frustrated her. She might be forced to take a trip to Scotland for research.

"Darro is a loyal guy. He would likely never say something was better than his granny's. You gotta love that about him. I wouldn't worry about it. Everyone loves your baking, Hedy," Mel assured her and Hedy smiled.

"I suppose I shouldn't be competitive with a dead Scottish grandmother, but baking is my claim to fame. I'll crack the secret to her recipe yet. Maybe I can ask Adelaide to commune with her in the spirit world and give me her secret?" Hedy asked with a laugh but the thought wasn't that far-fetched; she wasn't above asking a ghost to do a little reconnaissance for her. Maybe Adelaide would be able to reach dear old Granny Raith and get the secret at last. Of course, that would be if Adelaide would be willing and with that ghost, who could say.

# CHAPTER TWO

Yami Hayashi arrived in town just as it was turning to dusk. She was expected at the waystation, but first she had to meet the one who had hired her.

Her instructions were to go to a small park near the courthouse, which was easy enough to find; Enumclaw was a small town. There was a slab bench available, but Yami preferred to pace and watch; she did not want to get cornered unexpectedly. The park was mostly dark, despite the ring of Christmas lights illuminating the nearby streets. The sound of crow caws filtered through the cloudy dusk.

"I see you made it to this sleepy little hamlet." Lyssa's voice croaked out ofthe darkness but Yami could make out her figure standing next to a large tree. Yami had exceptional night vision but even so, Lyssa's form was little more than blackness. There was a scent of something rotting on the wind.

"Tokyo to Seattle to Enumclaw. I have been traveling a long while; you understand that you will be paying me extra for my inconvenience, yes?"

"You will be paid handsomely, don't worry about that. I need your particular skills to help me finish what I started in this town. I was thwarted by the waystation host and her friends; it was my fault for underestimating them. I won't make that mistake again." Lyssa spoke in a calm, measured way, but the grit of hatred simmered under the words.

"Fine. Tell me what you want, and I'll get the job done." Yami found the scent that seemed to envelope Lyssa growing in strength and she wanted to leave the park as quickly as she could. The sooner she finished the job, the sooner she could get back home. She was done with this kind of work; it was time to get out of the life.

"You'll go to the waystation and be my eyes and ears, reporting on what happens there. When the time is right, I'll have further instructions."

Yami nodded and turned to leave the park. She felt something on her shoulder, holding her back.

"But first, there is a small task I need you to perform. It will help set the wheels in motion." Lyssa's voice croaked in Yami's ear, bringing that smell too close, wrapping Yami in a putrid fog.

* * *

Though there was no set check-in time for a guest to arrive, most visitors came to the waystation by dinnertime. Travelers of all stripes seem to prefer company when they ate. Hedy kept an eye on the clock, but it was close to ten and still no visitor. The shop customers had dwindled down, no doubt the wet weather and the winter darkness contributing to that. Mel had gone home an hour earlier, leaving Hedy to wrap things up.

"Ready to close up shop?" Maurice, the chinchilla, wandered in from the kitchen where, by the looks of his fur, he had been sampling a bit of the trifle pudding.

"Yes, I think so. I'll switch the sign to closed, but I'll leave the door unlocked for a bit just in case our traveler arrives. In the meanwhile, I can get a bit more baking done for the morning." Maurice seemed satisfied with that response because he made no complaint; unusual for Maurice. He made his way to the entry and turned to head upstairs for the night.

Hedy almost asked him to stay, to keep her company, but she stopped herself. She knew a chinchilla of his advanced years needed his rest. She was feeling melancholy anyway and would likely be poor company for anyone at the moment.

The holidays were difficult. Hedy rarely had people around her for very long, and companions at Christmas were even scarcer. The last really happy Christmas had been in New Orleans, and that was a long time ago.

It wasn't that she didn't like Christmas. On the contrary, Hedy found the tradition and spectacle to be wonderful. But celebrating without friends or family could be challenging, especially when it seemed like all the world had loved ones at that time of the year. She had gotten used to having Bren around for the weeks that he stayed to watch for Lyssa. Now that he was gone, it reminded her that she had no one nearby with whom to share the season. It made her wistful.

"Enough of that, Miss Leckermaul. You have Zelda, Maurice, and Alice, you have Mel, you will see Anahita soon, and there is a new traveler coming. That should be enough to keep you busy." She heard her voice, but it sounded falsely hopeful even in her ears.

She was never very good at lying.

The front door bell tinkled and Hedy looked up to see a woman wrapped up against the weather standing in the doorway. She was tall and lithe, from what Hedy could see, and she had a backpack on her shoulder.

"Good evening. Are you Hedy Leckermaul?" The woman had a soft voice, with a Japanese accent. In the flickering candle light of the entryway, Hedy thought the traveler's eyes flashed green.

"Yes, welcome. Please come in. I wasn't sure you would make it tonight." Hedy came to meet her guest in the entryway and held out her hand to take the woman's wrap. The wool coat was soaked through. "My, I didn't know it was still raining that hard. I thought things had tapered down. You must be freezing. Please, come in and let me make you a hot drink while we get acquainted."

The woman nodded gratefully and followed Hedy into the shop, taking a seat near the counter. "Thank you, I would love some tea. I feel chilled to the bone tonight. My name is Yami Hayashi. I believe the Concierge told you of my arrival? I have my card to show you for identification."

Yami was a striking woman, with dark hair and a bit of a point to her face. Hedy saw in the light that her eyes were not green after all, but a lovely shade of dark brown, fringed with long eyelashes.

"Yes, you are my first traveler in a few months, and it is nice to have you here. Don't worry about the card; we don't stand on ceremony around here. I hope you will be with us for a while." Hedy hoped she didn't sound desperate when she said that, but it would be nice to have company again.

"My plans are not solid yet, but I do hope to impose on your kindness for a little while, if that is alright with you." Yami watched her host as she bustled behind the counter, brewing a pot of tea and placing cookies on a plate.

Yami wasn't sure she had ever seen a more absurd looking woman. Her host had impossibly out of style hair, with that sky-high up-do, and her clothes looked like something from another era. Yami tried to gauge Hedy's age and though her hair was white, her face and hands were youthful. She would guess she was in her mid-thirties, but she couldn't say for certain.

How could her employer have been thwarted

by this strange woman?

"Here we go. Hot tea and a few cookies for you. I suspect you've had a long day."

Yami accepted the tray with a smile and gave the teapot a delicate sniff; it was chamomile but Yami also detected apple and perhaps a bit of cinnamon.

"You have an amazing house, Miss Leckermaul. I've traveled the world, but I can't recall ever being in one quite like this." Yami poured a bit of tea into her cup and let the scent waft over her.

"Please, call me Hedy. Yes, it is an interesting house in its own right. When you add in all my curiosities...well, it does make it rather unusual." Hedy took the seat across from Yami, smoothing her apron as she spoke.

"The house is very large and looks old. Quite unlike the houses where I am from, to be sure." Yami took a sip of the tea; it was delicious. She would have to give the woman her due, she knew how to brew her tea.

"Where do you hail from, if you don't mind me asking?" It had been awhile since Hedy had more than a few words with someone other than Mel and she was genuinely interested in learning more about her guest.

"Japan. I was born in a small village in Okinawa, but I have spent almost all my life in Tokyo. I travel quite a bit for my work, but I am always anxious to get home. I enjoy the 'hustle and bustle,' I believe that is the phrase, of my city."

"Sounds hectic and very exciting to live in Tokyo. But do you ever crave the quiet of the countryside? Cities can be wonderful, but for me at least, I need some quiet time regularly or I feel a bit stifled." Hedy had lived in big cities before and she knew how impressive they could be, but also isolating.

"Oh, I find time to get away from the city. Either through my work or to visit friends who live in the Miyagi Prefecture. That is north of Tokyo, about four hours by car. It is nice to escape now and then. There is beautiful countryside in Japan."

Yami took another sip of her tea. Why was this woman so inquisitive about her life? Perhaps she wasn't as simple as she seemed.

"I must confess that I am not that familiar with Japan and its geography, but I hope to travel there one day. What would be interesting for a traveler in the Miyagi Prefecture?" Hedy watched the young woman as she sipped her tea, her eyes never leaving Hedy's face. She seemed rather intense for such small talk.

"There is a village there, Zao fox village. It is a refuge for foxes and people can go there to interact with them and feed them if they wish. It is rather famous." Yami finished her tea and placed the cup back on the plate.

"That sounds quite interesting indeed. I assume they are foxes that, for some reason, can't live in the wild? We have similar refuges here as well. Just south of here, actually, is such a sanctuary for wolves. Wolf Haven." Hedy watched the woman smile slightly but she said nothing more. Hedy was picking up the cue that her guest was ready to retire, and she rose from the table. No reason to press her tonight; there would be time for talking later.

"Yes, Zao is a place for those foxes who are not able to be in the wild, for one reason or another. It is a place I visit once or twice a year to catch up with my old friends." Yami rose from her seat and gathered her things.

"Well, I look forward to hearing more about Japan while you stay with us. You must be tired, so let me show you to your room. I have you in the room near the top of the stairs. You'll notice a large stone chaise in the room but pay that no mind. It belonged to a former guest. I left it there in case he needed to return. I think you will find the space comfortable."

Hedy led Yami out of the shop and down the hall toward the stairs. Hearing someone in the house besides the knocks and rattles of Adelaide would be nice again.

"I'm sure it will be just fine, thank you. I do appreciate your hospitality." Yami gazed around the hall at the objects covering every surface and slightly shook her head. She couldn't understand the need for such clutter. They passed through the wooden bramble gate and made their way up the stairs. Yami found the old-fashioned portraits that lined the walls to be depressing.

"Tomorrow, I will introduce you to the menagerie, to Mel, and to Adelaide. I'm afraid this house is likely more peculiar than you may have suspected." Hedy chuckled but her guest didn't join in.

"Oh, peculiar doesn't bother me at all. I've encountered many strange things in my travels, so it would take something truly unique to surprise me." Yami watched her host open the bedroom door and they bade each other good night. Yami closed the door behind her.

She hoped her employer would give her more direction beyond just watching and reporting on this house. What in the world could she want with this absurd baker?

# CHAPTER THREE

Thursday dawned drier than the day before, which for a Washington winter was a rare thing. Enumclaw was the gateway to a large ski resort and all anyone really cared about was how much snow was coming to the slopes. The weekend forecast called for a large snowstorm in the mountains, so Hedy expected skiers to start showing up in town, which might mean more business for her.

It was already stacking up to be a busy weekend. The town was having their annual Christmas market at the fairgrounds, which sounded a bit like the *Christkindlmarkt* she knew from her travels in Bavaria. There would be food, vendors, musicians and dancers, and a beer garden where they would have hot mulled wine. Hedy was one of the vendors, and for the occasion, she was making her grandmother's recipe for *Pfeffernüsse* , the German gingerbread famous at Christmastime.

Her guest was not up yet, and Mel wasn't due for an hour, so Hedy set to work gathering up the ingredients for the glazed gingerbread. Her grandmother's recipe called for honey, cream, and white pepper, among other secret spices. This would be the first time Hedy made the recipe to sell in the shop before. Perhaps this would be the beginning of a holiday tradition of her own.

Zelda, the tabby, meandered into the room, still licking her lips from her breakfast of kippers. Her coat was looking as well-groomed as always, but Hedy had noticed a bit of gray sprinkled among the black. Zelda would not appreciate the insinuation that she was aging; Maurice was the only one getting old as far as the cat was concerned.

"There's a bit of a ruckus on the back porch, Hedy. Something is out there pawing at the door. I can hear its nails scratching at the wood." Zelda didn't seem too intrigued by a mysterious visitor on the porch. If it wasn't a nice juicy vole, she had no use for it.

"Oh, I suspect it is a raccoon trying to get into our milk delivery box, but I will go check it out. Thank you, Zelda." Hedy left her ingredients on the counter and headed for the kitchen in the back. Maurice had not been down yet this morning as his breakfast wasn't touched, but it looked like Alice, the magpie, had come and gone for the day.

Hedy heard the scratching and tried looking through the glass at the top of the door for a glimpse at the visitor. Unfortunately, whatever was making the noise was too close to the door; she could see nothing. Hedy made a point of making noise as she unlocked the door and gingerly opened it. If it was a raccoon, she thought it might scamper off at the sound of activity. Hedy peered out the opened door and saw Ren, the fox, pacing in front of her.

"I am glad you finally came to the door. I have trouble and I need your help." Ren stopped pacing and sat in front of Hedy, looking worried. Ren's previous visit inside the house had given Hedy the ability to understand his speech due to Circe's staff, which hung in the hallway. A side benefit to Hedy's strange collection.

"What can I do for you, Ren? Do you want to come inside?" Hedy suspected he would rather stay right where he was; as a wild creature, being inside a human's home would likely be an uncomfortable place.

"No, I am fine here. But I do need your help. I fear the humans will be hunting me and my kind, and I have no way to stop it."

"What has happened?" Hedy had no idea what could be causing the fox such distress.

"Last night, there were attacks at several farms. Mostly chickens, some goats, and even a few sheep. The attacks look like the work of a fox, but no fox near the human farms was involved - they know better than to provoke a reaction from the humans. Foxes survive close to civilization because we know how to stay out of human business. Whatever fox or creature attacked these farms last night is going to bring havoc on the rest of us."

Ren started pacing again, clearly unable to sit still with all this happening.

"What would you like me to do?" Hedy was sympathetic, surely, but she didn't really know what she could do to help the fox.

"If you can, tell the farmers not to trap foxes. Let them know that the foxes will deal with it themselves. We will handle this danger."

Hedy tried to keep the skepticism off her face as he spoke.

"I'm afraid that might be difficult. They won't understand that I am having a conversation with you about it all. Maybe if you can find the culprit and put a quick stop to it, the farmers won't have time to get organized?"

Hedy wanted to help, but she really didn't see what she could do. The last thing she could do was go around telling the farmers of Enumclaw that a fox told her to spread the word. People thought she was strange as it is.

"We are looking, even now, but you don't know how quickly they will turn on us for this. They think we've harmed their livelihood. They will have traps out all over the place by the end of today, mark my words." Ren didn't know why he expected this human to be any more helpful than other humans in the past. As always, foxes were on their own.

"Ren, I'll think about how I can help, I really will. I don't know any of these farmers personally, but maybe there is a way that I can help influence them, so they don't hunt any foxes. I promise I will think about it and try to help."

It was the best that Hedy could offer, and she could tell that the fox was disappointed. The thought of not having a solution to Ren's problem bothered her. Hedy was the one everyone turned to for help and she took pride in that. A feeling of failure gnawed in her belly.

Ren gave her a curt nod and left the porch without another word. She wondered if she would ever see him again.

Hedy closed the door and pondered the situation. Even if what Ren said was true and a fox wasn't behind the attacks, something was, and the farmers had to put a stop to it. The best scenario would be that whatever it was had moved on and the attacks would stop, so the farmers wouldn't be inclined to continue looking for the culprit. She had promised Ren she would think about a solution and she planned to keep her word. She would mull it all over while she was working on her gingerbread.

Hedy went back to the shop trying to solve a puzzle on how a human baker could help a fox from the traps of angry farmers.

✻ ✻ ✻

"Good morning, Hedy. Looks like a nicer day today." Mel arrived a short while later, wrapped up in a down jacket and a knitted cap. Under all her layers, she was wearing a red plaid jumper, which was definitely more in keeping with Hedy's vintage style than Mel's more utilitarian look.

"Nice dress, Mel. Where did you get that?" Hedy admired the flared hem and the two brass buttons at the shoulder straps. Mel wore it over a dark green turtleneck, and she looked adorable, although Hedy thought a big poinsettia hair flower would finish things off nicely.

"My mother bought it for me. She went by that new store I mentioned, The Red Bat, and found it. She thinks I need to branch out from my basic black." Mel looked down at the dress, still unsure if she could pull of something with this much pattern.

"Well, it looks wonderful. Your mother made a good choice. I will definitely have to go check out that shop. Once you are settled, we are working on German gingerbread today for the Saturday market."

Mel stashed her coat and cap on the rack and hid her backpack behind the front counter. She found her apron on the hook by the kitchen doorway, and after a thorough hand scrubbing at the sink, she was ready to work.

"I had a visit from Ren this morning. Sounds like there is trouble in his world." Hedy shared the story of the attacks on the farms as she mixed the ingredients in the bowl.

"People around here take those kinds of attacks seriously. I wouldn't be surprised if there are fox traps all over their land by nightfall. Ren will have to be careful." Mel watched as Hedy took the sticky mixture and turned it out on a large sheet of plastic wrap, carefully wrapping it up into a large disk for the refrigerator.

"That is Ren's fear, and he wants me to help stop it. I honestly don't know what I can do for him. There is no way I can go to one of these farmers and tell them a fox told me that they didn't do this, so please don't set traps." Hedy was ready to combine the ingredients again for another batch and she demonstrated to Mel as she spoke. They would likely need five full batches for the market.

"Unfortunately, fox hunting season runs from autumn into the early spring. There is no legal reason why they can't hunt them, if they think they are a danger." Mel had family members who had small farms and she was sympathetic to the destruction that a creature, such as a fox, could cause.

"Well, I told him I would try to think of a way I could help. I really don't know what I can do, but I will keep my word."

"My uncle owns a small farm on the edge of town. I'll ask if he had any issues and see what I can find out. If nothing else, maybe we can at least find out what measures they are planning to take so we can warn Ren." Mel started melting the butter, sugar and honey on the stove, giving it all a stir as she mirrored Hedy's actions. They would have the five batches prepared and chilling in no time.

"Thank you, that definitely would be helpful. I'll ask Alice to keep watch while she is out and about; perhaps she will see something that might be of help as well." Even these small plans made Hedy feel like she was keeping her promise to the fox, and she felt better about it all.

The landline telephone interrupted their thoughts with its sharp ring. Hedy had a rotary phone and an old answering machine as her communication tools. She knew she would eventually have to move to a smartphone, but she didn't like the idea of having the telephone always at her side.

"That ring always startles me. It sounds like something out of an old movie." Mel found the phone hilarious and even more so that Hedy hadn't transitioned to a more modern age, especially as a business owner. She hoped to help Hedy with her first computer before she left for college in the spring.

Hedy wiped her hands quickly and grabbed the receiver before the second ring was done.

"Good morning, The Gingerbread Hag. How can I help you?" She never liked the sound of her voice, especially on the phone.

"Is this Miss Leckermaul speaking?" The voice on the other end had a thick French accent. She knew immediately that it was the Concierge.

"Yes, this is Miss Leckermaul. Waystation 1167." She guessed that the Concierge was calling her about another traveler.

"Waystation 1167, you will be receiving an inspection. Prepare for the arrival of Raluca Vaduva. She will be at your waystation by the end of the day." The line clicked off and Hedy was left holding the receiver, looking at it in wonderment.

"Who was that? Do we have an order?" Mel watched Hedy hang up the receiver and walk back toward the counter.

"No, that was the waystation Concierge. It seems we are going to be receiving an inspection." Hedy wasn't quite sure what to make of the revelation.

"Oh, is that usual? What is it that this person inspects?" Mel had come to terms with the concept of the waystation; her girlfriend was one of the travelers who used them as safe harbors as she journeyed from place to place.

"No, it's quite unusual. When a waystation opens for the first time, there is a local inspection by the nearest waystation host. In my case, because I had apprenticed in New Orleans, when I moved to Portland and opened my first waystation, the host from southern Oregon came up and signed off on the house. It is rather an informal thing, just checking that the facility is up to standards. After that, waystations are left to their own devices, unless there is a problem."

Hedy wondered if the recent issue with Lyssa had caused the Concierge to be concerned about the safety of her waystation.

"Did they tell you who is coming? Do you know them?" Mel thought Hedy looked worried, which seemed surprising for something as simple as an inspection. Everything in Hedy's house seemed just right to her.

"Yes. Raluca Vaduva is coming. I've never met her - no one that I know has met her; I think that she is high up in the Concierge management. They are not just sending a host to check on me. This is serious." Hedy couldn't imagine why someone like Raluca Vaduva would be coming all the way to Enumclaw to inspect her waystation. Would she be shut down? Permanently?

"Well, what can we do to get ready? I mean the house already looks great, so I don't know that there is anything left there, but whatever you think we need to do today, just say the word." Mel had started on another batch of dough, now that she had the knack of it.

"No, we don't need to do anything other than go about our day. She'll be here soon enough and then we'll see what she says. Oh, I should probably warn you, though." Hedy watched as Mel's face started to blanch. "If rumors are true, Raluca is a bit unusual looking. I don't want you to be startled when you see her. By all accounts, you'll know her the minute you see her." Hedy started working on her own dough, hoping the routine would calm her nerves.

"What does she look like?" Mel wondered how much more unusual could this Raluca be, compared to Hedy's own rather striking appearance.

"Well, again, I have only heard rumors. But Raluca is a Moroaica, and because she is so long-lived, she will look quite ancient. She's also very short. Or so I am told." Raluca Vaduva was something of a mystery, rumors and stories about her were known throughout the network. She sounded like quite the formidable woman.

"What's a Moroaica?" Mel tried to say the word carefully, unsure exactly how to pronounce it.

"I've heard differing origins, but the one I believe is the one I learned in New Orleans. A Moroaica is a female mortal vampire, the child of two Strigoi - undead vampires. Legend has it that the Moroi live long lives, but they are mortal, and they do not need to feed on humans. How that works exactly, I don't know. They are incredibly rare, at least that is the rumor. But we don't need to fear Raluca. They wouldn't send her if she was a danger to us. At least I hope that is the case anyway." She had never encountered anyone like Raluca before, so she was going on faith.

"Well, and here I thought this was just going to be a boring Thursday, making cookies and reading up on linear algebra. Imagine instead meeting an ancient mortal vampire, coming here to inspect your house. Crazy."

Mel was laughing but she meant what she said. It was crazy to her that such things happened all around her and she had no idea before. It's like she had been asleep and now suddenly awoke to a world where everything was inside out.

"Like I said, don't worry. Whatever Raluca wants, she will be dealing with me. If you can help me get the gingerbread ready for the market, that will be a big help. Also, I think the tree might be dry enough now to bring into the house, so I'll need some help getting it into its stand. It's just another Thursday." Hedy chuckled and worked on her batch of dough, getting it wrapped up in the plastic wrap. One more batch and then into the freezer they went for an hour or so.

Whatever the day would bring, she'd deal with it as it came. Even if that meant a mortal vampire.

# CHAPTER FOUR

As much as the visit from Raluca was on her mind, Hedy scarcely had time to think about it. Thursday was shaping up to be a busy day. Tonight, there was an event out at the tree farm near Mount Enumclaw and it seemed many parents wanted treats to bring along. Mel and Hedy were kept busy filling orders for Krampus cookies, peppermint bark brownies, and bags of reindeer kibble, which was just Hedy's name for chocolate dipped pretzel bits covered in sprinkles. The morning was fast becoming the afternoon and they hadn't even had time to set up the tree.

"Is it alright with you if I leave a little early today? My family is going out to the tree farm tonight; we are meeting up with my uncle and my cousin, Dylan." Mel knew Hedy wouldn't refuse such a request.

"Of course. Sounds like fun. Will there be caroling and hot cider out there?" Hedy had never gone to a tree farm for her Christmas tree. She had either lived in a city and found a lot on the corner, or she had tromped out into the woods and found one. The idea of growing a crop of Christmas trees amused her.

"Yes, and a hay ride and a maze. My cousin is twelve and he loves the maze. Personally, I hate them. Plus they are never very hard to figure out." Mel's mathematical mind found mazes an easy challenge, but she didn't like the slight claustrophobia that they induced.

"Well, have a marvelous time. Be sure to take some treats to share with your cousin. We might actually have a pause right now if we want to get the tree set up. I can work on decorating it tonight, assuming there is time before Raluca arrives." Mel and Hedy went to the porch to get the tree and found Darro working in the yard; Hedy hadn't expected to see him again until next week.

"What brings you here, Darro? I thought we were on maintenance mode now for the garden?" Darro came up to the porch when he saw them both come out.

"Good morning to ye both. I thought I would swing in and set up a few snares in your garden today. There has been a rash of fox attacks out on the farms and since the blighters have caused such damage to the hens, we should do our part to catch them."

Darro was surprised to see both Mel and Hedy gasp.

"Oh, Darro, no. We need those snares taken out right away. No traps in the garden, please. This yard needs to be a haven for those who need it."

"A'right, I'll do as ye ask. But foxes are predators and they might strike your own cat if given the chance. Ye don't want to encourage them to take up residence. They are no better than vermin, Hedy." Darro thought that for two sensible women, they seemed awfully worked up at the thought of snares for creatures that would kill chickens. Hedy's own neighbor had a small chicken coop just a few doors down. He shook his head at the foolishness.

"Please take them out right away and we'll agree to disagree on the merit of foxes. Thank you, Darro." Mel and Hedy looked meaningfully at each other, and Darro scratched his head before heading back down the stairs. It must be another strange situation in this house; the whole lot of them were radge in Darro's opinion.

"As you say. I'll hop to it. Do ye need a hand with the tree?" The women had it by the trunk and were lifting it toward the front door.

"No, I think we have it. The snares are the priority. Thanks for the offer, though." They wrangled it inside and shut the door behind them.

"Pure radge, the pair of 'em," Darro muttered under his breath as he set off to undo all the work he had just done.

"Well, that was close. I'm glad we saw him setting those up," Mel spoke through a face full of fir needles. The tree was large and quite a challenge to move through the hall without striking any of the curios that lined the walls.

"Yes. I'm sure he meant well, but he definitely should have checked with me before setting those up. Even if this situation with the foxes wasn't happening, I wouldn't have wanted those snares set up, if for no other reason than Zelda likes to go out hunting in the garden." Hedy could well imagine the rashing she would get if Zelda found her tail nipped in a trap.

The women managed to walk the tree toward the back of the hall, where Hedy had the stand set up to receive it. It was definitely a large tree, probably larger than any Hedy had decorated before, but it suited the size of the hall well. They lifted in tandem and managed to get it set into the stand. Luckily, Hedy had purchased a more modern stand that allowed for an easy tilting to make sure the tree was centered straight. After only a few twists of the securing rods and a few directions of "more to the left" from Mel, the tree was straight and braced.

"Perfect, thank you. Don't you love that smell? Fresh trees have such a delicious smell. Puts me in mind to make some juniper coffee cake, with a bit of cranberry glaze. Thank you, Mel. I never would have been able to get the tree in by myself." For some reason, this year Hedy seemed to be finding herself in situations where being alone would be a hindrance. Perhaps the universe was trying to tell her something.

"No problem. It may take me a bit to get all this sap off my fingers, but it is a gorgeous tree. I'm excited to see what you do with it."

The bell tinkled before Hedy could share her plans for decorations. It was probably for the best; the tree would be better seen than described.

"Oh, what a lovely tree. Smells just like a tree farm in here." Mrs. Wilson came toward the shop, meeting Hedy and Mel at the doorway.

"Good to see you, Mrs. Wilson. I hope the grandchildren are doing well." Hedy enjoyed seeing Mrs. Wilson on her trips to babysit her grandkids. She always stopped to bring them treats.

"Oh, yes, they are quite excited for Christmas. They are on their best behavior, what with the Elf on the Shelf watching them." Mrs. Wilson saw the blank look on Hedy's face and explained. "You know, the elf that arrives after Thanksgiving and keeps an eye on the kids, reporting their behavior to Santa? Surely, you've seen those dolls at the store?"

Hedy shook her head. She could say with certainty she had never seen any kind of elf sitting on a shelf.

"I bet most parents rue the day they brought the elf into the house. They have to keep thinking up clever settings and treats all December for the elf to surprise the kids. Sounds like a ton of work to me." Mel wasn't trying to be bah-humbug about the elf but who needed that kind of pressure. Wasn't an old advent calendar with the daily chip of chocolate good enough?

"I'll have to check into this; I only know

the Nisse from Scandinavia, with their adorable gnome hats and long beards. In fact, I probably have a few scattered in the hallway that I picked up from a trip to Oslo a few years back." Hedy went behind the counter and picked up an empty box to fill with treats for Mrs. Wilson.

"You always are so quirky, Hedy, with your style and your strange collection. I swear you are like something out of another place and time. A veritable fish out of water." Mrs. Wilson laughed and handed Hedy the money for her goodies. She couldn't imagine being so out of touch with everyday things. Mrs. Wilson took her box and with a "Merry Christmas," she was out the door.

Hedy said nothing, yet Mel could tell that Mrs. Wilson's words had upset her. "For what it is worth, Hedy, you aren't a fish out of water. Most of us have things we like that aren't what other people consider typical. How many teenagers my age do you think read Algebra for fun?" Mel herself had many times felt like a fish out of water with her classmates but she didn't want to compound the situation by telling that to Hedy.

"It's okay, Mel. It isn't the first time someone has called me quirky when they really mean weird. And you know what? I am weird. I am a strange person to anyone looking. I mean, not too many people today are sporting a beehive hairdo, collecting macabre relics, and talking to animals. Come on, let's just be honest."

Hedy placed the trays back in the case and went

over to the large copper tureen for hot water; she needed a cup of tea.

"So, what if all that is true? What makes weird somehow bad? I think weird is wonderful. Certainly, Anahita could be classified as weird, and I wouldn't have her any other way." Mel started wiping down the already clean counter for something to do.

"As I said, it's alright. I'm not about to go changing myself now; this is who I am. Every once in a while, it stings a little to be so obviously reminded that I am often on the outside looking in. But that is neither here nor there. We have to get things wrapped up for the day so you can get out of here and enjoy the tree farm. And I have a visitor to prepare for." Hedy had the pot filled with water and she added several scoops of a mixture of fragrant tea leaves.

She wished she had taken the opportunity to learn to read the leaves when she lived in New Orleans with Delphine; she could use a bit of insight into her future. She would have liked to have called Delphine for advice, but they hadn't spoken in years.

"Okay, Hedy. I have the donuts ready to bake and we have a full stock of peppermint bark and reindeer kibble. What's next?"

Hedy gave the pot a swirl and then wrapped it up in a sweater cozy to keep it warm while it steeped. She wished she could share with Mel what she was feeling, the sense of dread and unknown that seemed to have settled into her heart. She refused to burden Mel with her worries, whether they were founded or not. Mel was so happy these days. Instead, she smiled.

"If you can play some Christmas music on your phone, I could use some help making rum balls. After that, go enjoy yourself." Mel nodded and the two set to work.

* * *

The last of the rum balls rolled and placed on trays, Mel headed out the door, leaving Hedy with her thoughts. Whenever she was feeling uneasy, Hedy usually would try a new recipe. Today, she thought perhaps she could keep tweaking on her scones to see if she could impress Darro. Surely something in her library of cookbooks would have a hint as to what made Scottish scones unique.

She headed upstairs, confident that she would hear the front door bell if anyone came inside. She'd scour her library of recipes to see what she could learn to compete with the scones of a dead Scottish grandmother.

The library, dim even in summer mornings, was shadowy and cold. Hedy lit candle after candle so that she would be able to actually read whatever she might find. Soon enough the room was full of soft warm glow; it did nothing to change the chill in the air, but that was as likely due to Adelaide as to any problem with the furnace.

"Adelaide, I'm looking for a recipe. Hopefully I am not disturbing you." Hedy didn't know what a ghost might be doing where she could be disturbed, but it never hurt to be polite.

The candle flames flickered slightly in response.

"I don't suppose you know any secrets of Scottish scone makers, do you? Your family was Swedish, I believe." Hedy ran her finger along the spines of several books, looking for a volume of The Best of Traditional British Cooking. She wondered if she had loaned it out to a neighbor, back when she lived in Portland. "I'm trying to impress Darro by replicating his Granny Raith's scone recipe."

The book was definitely not where it should have been. The question was who she would have loaned it to.

"Sweets," Adelaide's voice was soft but unmistakable in the quiet.

"Yes, scones can be sweets, especially with Devonshire cream and jam." Hedy placed her forefinger into the space where the book should have been. Maybe she had it up in her reading pile in the attic?

"I like..." Adelaide spoke again, pausing. Hedy waited but she didn't finish the sentence.

"I like them too, Adelaide. We have that in common." The candle flames flickered strongly, and Hedy worried they would be blown out.

"But teeth, sharp." Adelaide's voice was now worried sounding, almost too soft to hear.

"Sharp teeth? Whose? Are you talking about Ren?" Hedy waited and the candles continued to flicker. Did Adelaide know about the attacks on the farms? How could she? Hedy felt frustrated that she couldn't just get a straight answer from the ghost."Adelaide? Are you here still? Are you warning me or are we still talking about sweets?"

She needed a better way to communicate with her spectral roommate.

"Here. Watch...for teeth." Her voice trailed off and the candle flames went still again.

Whatever the ghost was trying to tell her, it was as cryptic and infuriating as ever.

# CHAPTER FIVE

Yami was not one for rising or shining. She preferred late nights and lazy mornings. Her room was adequate, certainly better than many of the places she had stayed for assignments, but it didn't suit her taste. She preferred minimalism and sleek lines; this room was all Victorian fluff and bother. Be that as it may, she slept surprisingly well given she was in a strange place and unsure as to what threats there might be. She managed to sleep through most of the morning before opening her eyes to the filtered light coming through the window.

Her ears immediately picked up the sound of rustling downstairs. No doubt her host would be at work in her shop, which suited Yami just fine. She wasn't in the mood for more small talk.

More and more, she wasn't finding this life fulfilling, and she kept longing to return home to Tokyo. Sure, the money was good, but she had plenty for now and her needs were small other than her lovely and incredibly expensive downtown apartment. She might just make this her last job. Her ties to the Tokyo underworld had been severed, quite literally, last year in a turf war and that left her without anyone demanding she work. She had only taken this job because Lyssa could be very persuasive.

Yami stretched and lightly left the bed, tussling her bobbed hair as she did so. Lyssa had asked her for regular reports on the activities in this house and so far, there was nothing to report. The host baked, and that appeared to be it. Yami had thought it was some kind of cover for more devious activity, but after one day in the house, it was easy to believe that Hedy was in fact, just a baker. Sure, she was also a waystation host, but there seemed to be nothing else of note about her, nothing sinister or even interesting for Yami to report about. She had to wonder if Lyssa knew what she was doing with this assignment. Why did she need Yami to be her eyes and ears on this ordinary woman?

She unplugged her phone from the charger and checked the latest news from The Japan Times. There wasn't as much Christmas in the news in Japan as in the west; celebrating the new year was by far the bigger holiday. Yami had to admit that she liked to be on a job during December so she could visit somewhere with the traditions of the season. Despite her preference for empty spaces, she did find a fully trimmed tree to be rather pleasing.

"Alright, time to begin." She set down the phone and put on her usual work attire of black leggings and a dark grey tunic. She gave her appearance a quick scan in the mirror and then headed down to the hustle and bustle of the house. Time to keep her eyes and ears open.

She made her way down the stairs, finding a huge fir tree now sitting in the hallway by the stairs. The scent reminded her of her work last night and she smiled. There was also the scent of baking, with the spices of cinnamon and cardamom easy to pick out. Yami's keen nose also found the warm smell of rum and she checked her watch to see if it was too early for a nip. She entered the shop to find Hedy behind the counter with a younger girl who was rolling balls of dough in her hands.

"Ah, there is our guest. Yami, please come meet Mel, a friend of the house." Hedy had looked sad when Yami entered the room and though she was smiling now, she wondered what had been happening before.

Yami approached the counter and gave a small bow to the young woman. They both had similar bobbed hairstyles. The girl was shorter than Yami and gave off the impression of someone bookish and quiet.

"Pleased to meet you, Yami. I just help out in the shop. Right now, Hedy has me rolling rum balls and I can't even sample them." Mel gave Hedy a smile and Yami could tell that the girl was trying to cheer her up.

"It is my pleasure to meet you, Mel. The scent

from the shop is quite intoxicating, including those rum balls. I may just have to break my rule of no sweets and sample a bit. Everything smells so wonderful."

For the first time, Hedy looked appalled. "No sweets! What kind of a rule is that? My goodness, what would ever compel you to have that kind of rule?" Hedy paused in her work to fetch a plate for Yami.

"In general, I don't have much of a sweet tooth. My tastes run to more savory flavors. I also find that too much sugar leaves me feeling..." she was searching for the English word for *teimei*, "sluggish. Yes, it makes me sluggish. I prefer to feel sharp." Yami accepted the plate and took a seat near the counter so she could continue to watch them work.

"Yes, I suppose too much of anything is bad, including sugar. I would find it very hard to face every day though if I had to bar myself from such a simple pleasure. I probably would benefit from adopting that rule now and then." Hedy chuckled and returned to the rum balls.

Yami took a bite of the cinnamon roll that was shaped like a snail and she had to admit, it was delicious. The baker definitely knew her craft.

"So, what is on the schedule for you today, Yami? Hopefully you will be with us on Saturday so you can visit the Christmas market. There should be a good assortment of vendors and some festive performances. I'll have a booth there."

"Yes, I suspect I will still be here, and it sounds quite interesting. As for today, I thought I would just take a rest day and stay around the house, if you don't mind." Yami took another bite of her cinnamon roll and smiled appreciatively at Hedy.

"Of course, feel free to putter about as you wish. If you wouldn't mind, I could use a hand decorating the tree today. Don't feel like you need to say yes, but if you are so inclined, I'd be happy for the help." Hedy watched Yami nod in response since her mouth was full. She very much liked the idea of having help decorating the tree.

"Great. As soon as Mel and I finish these rum balls, she will be leaving, and we can get to the tree. I have several boxes of lights and ornaments in the garage that I'll bring in and we can get to work." Hedy heard a tinge of excitement in her own voice and she hoped she wasn't coming across as too desperate. The last thing she wanted to do was make her guest feel uncomfortable.

"That sounds delightful. I can say this may be the first time I have ever decorated a tree. I'm often traveling in December and when I am home, I don't decorate my apartment. This will be a first." Yami saw the young girl smile, almost in gratitude, and she guessed that Hedy might be lonely this Christmas season. Yami would have to investigate that to see what advantage it might provide.

A few more customers came in and Yami watched them order some of the Krampus cookies or fox tail donuts, which Yami found particularly distasteful; as if anyone should want to eat a dismembered fox tail. In between customers the rum balls were complete, and Mel was preparing to leave for the day. It would just be Hedy and Yami, at least until Hedy's next visitor arrived.

" I'll see you tomorrow." Mel said, waving goodbye as she headed out the front door. She was relieved that Hedy had some company for the rest of the day, if for no other reason than to take her mind off the inspection with the visitor. Mel had to admit that she was excited at the prospect of an evening with nothing strange or unusual to prepare for, just selecting a Christmas tree with her family.

The women headed to the detached garage to bring in Hedy's decorations for the tree. Yami was glad of the opportunity to look around for anything of interest for Lyssa, but the garage looked like a dustier version of the house, with boxes and curios lining the walls. Though there was a blue Corvair parked in the center. Hedy maneuvered through the bric-a-brac until she found what she was looking for. There were three larger cardboard boxes marked "Xmas" on the side.

"Here we are, this should be everything. I don't think they are especially heavy, just bulky." Hedy picked up a box, testing the weight, and found it was manageable. Yami took a box from the stack and they headed back toward the house. The sky looked ominous, as if yesterday's rain was on its way back.

"I hope the rain holds off until after Mel's event tonight." Hedy hurried up the porch stairs and held the door open for Yami.

"Wouldn't it be lucky if you were a weather witch and you could give her a little help?" Yami smiled as she set the box down by the tree and Hedy laughed.

"Oh, no, no powers here. There have been times that I have wished that I did have powers, but no, the best I can do is just keep my fingers crossed for her." Hedy headed back to the garage for the final box, leaving Yami to cross witchcraft off her mental list.

There had to be something about Hedy that made her worthy of Lyssa's attention, and more dangerously, her wrath.

Yami opened the box and found strings of lights, rather haphazardly coiled, leaving them a bit tangled and difficult to extract. She began carefully drawing out a strand, trying to keep it from getting caught on the other bulbs while Hedy returned with the final box.

"Hopefully the lights aren't too tangled. We'll need to put them on the tree first. I'm hoping four strings of lights will be enough; this tree is a bit larger than my last trees have been." Hedy squatted down next to Yami and began pulling out a string of her own. With a bit of lifting and prodding, they managed to get all the strings out and into four separate piles. Hedy plugged in the first string and it lit up in a shimmering silver glow. One by one, they plugged the other strings into the first until they were all connected in one long line.

With a pattern not discernible to Yami, Hedy wove the lights among the branches, starting at the base and tucking the strings in deep, near the trunk of the tree. It wasn't long before the entire tree was lit with the silver glow.

"OK, that should work. That looks like enough lights, don't you think?" Hedy glanced over at Yami who was nodding slowly. "Now the fun part. Let's get the ornaments on." Hedy opened a second box and began drawing out what appeared to be glittering spiders and webs.

"Hedy, forgive the question, but is it common to decorate with spiders?" Yami asked as Hedy opened her hand and offered one of the glass spider ornaments to Yami for placing on the tree. It was gorgeous, if quite strange.

"Well, I guess it depends on what part of the world you are in. In America, yes, I would say it is unusual to have spiders on a Christmas tree. In Ukraine or Poland, most trees have a least one spiderweb, though I doubt most trees end up looking like mine. There is an old story about a poor family who couldn't decorate their tree, so the spiders covered it in beautiful webs. I have always loved the story, so I collect spider themed ornaments."

Hedy had a large ruby red spider with glittering green legs in her hand and she was looking for a sturdy branch that could support the weight.

"You seem to have traveled quite a bit. What's your story?" Besides trying to find out more for her assignment, Yami found herself genuinely wanting to know about the strange woman pulling jewel spiders from her ornament box.

"I have traveled, yes. It was something I wanted to do since I was a teenager. Life at home wasn't always good so the first chance I had to take off for another place, I grabbed it. I've visited and even lived in a lot of wonderful places, and I hope to do more traveling at some point in the future. For now, I am happy hosting the waystation and having the travelers come to me."

"Did your work take you to all these places? I mean, not to be crass, but being a world traveler is an expensive hobby." Yami hoped she wasn't being offensive but she didn't know how Hedy could afford such activity on a baker's salary.

"No, it's a valid question. I'm fortunate in that my family has left me well situated. I am not rich, but I have what I need to support my life. I had an ancestor or two who were rather canny with their money and it helped the rest of us down the line." Hedy wasn't exactly embarrassed by the conversation, but she felt like it made her sound as if she wasn't able to support herself, that she needed the family trust money to survive. It certainly was a help, but she had always worked, since she was eighteen years old.

"I understand. And, of course, I meant no disrespect. I was just curious about how you managed to visit so many places. Your home is a monument to travel." Yami glanced around the hall at all the curiosities lining the walls and gave a broad smile, which she hoped Hedy interpreted as appreciation.

"I have been lucky to visit many of the places I have always wanted to see and to bring back some interesting things as mementos. I'm not sure if my travel bug made me a collector or the other way around. In any event, if I gather any more items, I will need a bigger house." Hedy laughed as she rustled near the bottom of the box of ornaments. "Just a few more ornaments and then I have to figure out how to get the star on top."

"Oh, I can handle that for you. I can be quite nimble." Yami found the star and quickly hopped up onto the top of the step ladder. She stood on one foot, almost en pointe, and reached her arm high above her head. She had just enough height to bring the star to the top of the tree and settle it gently. With a hop, she was off the ladder and back on the ground.

"You must have been a dancer at some point. That was beyond nimble, Yami. Thank you."

Her guest bowed slightly and then stood back to admire the tree. Yami had to admit that the effect of all the jeweled spiders and silver spider webs was rather breathtaking against the cold silver lights in the branches.

"Wait until you see it with the other lights turned low. It really is a beautiful effect." Hedy placed the last ornament, a filigree silver web, in an empty space near the top, and then she too stepped back to take it all in. As much work as it was, the tree was always worth the effort.

"It's lovely, Hedy. Thank you for letting me assist you. I'm not one for taking pictures usually but if you wouldn't mind, I'd like to get a picture of you with the tree as a memento." Yami always tried to take photos of her subjects while working on a job; they came in handy, though she had to be scrupulous in deleting them from her phone's memory once the job was done.

"Of course. I'll take off my apron if you don't mind." Hedy removed the polka dot apron and Yami could better see the corduroy jumper and mustard yellow turtleneck underneath. She honestly couldn't imagine where Hedy found her clothing.

"Okay, here we go. Ichi…ni…san." As Yami reached three and snapped the picture, the doorbell rang, startling both women. They both turned to find a visitor unlike anyone either had ever seen before.

The woman seemed to be less than five feet tall and her frame was rather thin, although she was swathed in layers of black wool wrappings. The one hand she had exposed looked ancient, with deep crevasses and long, claw-like nails painted in pearlized violet. Her face was dominated by an enormous pair of dark black sunglasses.

"Hedy Leckermaul." The woman spoke sharply and without preamble.

"Yes, that is me." Hedy stepped away from the tree, coming a bit closer to the figure by the door.

"I am Raluca Vaduva. I am here for your inspection."

# CHAPTER SIX

The small figure faced the two women with a stern expression, giving Hedy the impression that she had already failed in some fashion. Hedy hadn't mentioned any of this to Yami and now she would have some explaining to do.

"Yami, we have a visitor from the Concierge head office. I'll be closing up the shop early so that I can assist Miss Vaduva with her inspection." Hedy stepped forward to close the door behind Raluca and she caught the unmistakable scent of metal - like copper or iron. She closed the door and switched the sign, gesturing for Raluca to enter the bakery.

Yami watched the two leave the entry. What an interesting development to share with Lyssa. She'd have to hover in the hall on some pretext so she could be sure to learn more about this inspection. Perhaps the tree needed some adjusting.

Hedy watched as Raluca began to slowly unwrap herself from her black woolen pashmina. The figure under the wool was even smaller than Hedy had first thought. Raluca emerged in a dark lavender Chanel suit, with a string of impossibly perfect and large pearls around her tiny neck that were no doubt real. Her jet-black hair was short and perfectly smooth.

"Miss Vaduva, may I offer you some refreshment? Coffee or tea, perhaps?" Hedy gestured again, this time for Raluca to take a seat.

"I very much doubt you have the type of beverage I would most enjoy. But a cup of tea will do." Raluca settled lightly into a seat and watched Hedy with a piercing gaze.

"I have not had a Moroaica visit before and the notice of your visit was quite short. If I had known, I could have been prepared with some blood from the butcher." Hedy was concentrating on the tea and didn't notice the amusement on Raluca's face.

"What makes you think I meant blood as a beverage? I was speaking of țuică, a Romanian spirit made from plums. You clearly have more to learn about Moroi." The old woman watched Hedy bring the tea pot and two cups to the table.

"My apologies for my ignorance. As I said, Moroi are unknown to me. When I have a traveler come, I like to know as much as I can to make sure they feel most welcome. I've made a pot of Earl Grey. Would you like something to eat to go with it?" Hedy didn't know what, if anything, that Moroi ate so she thought it best to make no specific offers.

"The tea will be sufficient for now, thank you.

By way of education, Moroi, such as myself, have both human and vampiric qualities. I eat food, I age, albeit extremely slowly, and I can be out in the daylight if I am well protected. Unlike my parents, who were Strigoi and were created by another vampire, I was born and have many human tendencies. And a few not so human." Raluca chuckled and accepted Hedy's cup, waiving off the sugar or cream.

"Thank you for the information. I'll remember it if I ever have another Moroi come to visit me." Hedy added a scoop of sugar to her own cup, which Raluca noticed and appeared to judge.

"I very much doubt you will meet another. We are a rare thing. I myself have only met two others in my lifetime, and I was born four hundred years ago." Raluca took a slight sip of the tea and found it acceptable.

"Well, then I am especially honored to have you visiting my waystation." Hedy thought she detected a small smile of satisfaction on Raluca's face.

"I don't know if you should be 'honored' as you say. My visit was prompted by concern at the highest levels of the network. It says much that a tiny town such as this comes under our scrutiny." Raluca took another sip and then set the cup down.

"How can I alleviate your concerns?" Hedy thought it best to get to the point straight away. What did she need to do to continue to be a waystation?

"We were concerned to hear that two of your guests were involved in a local matter with a petty arsonist. In fact, both of your guests were placed directly in harm's way and, if the reports are true, the undine almost died. That is unacceptable." Raluca's black eyes stared at Hedy with an unwavering gaze. She was here for answers.

"Yes, it is true that the waystation had a situation a few months back. There was a person in town who was kidnapping women and burning down buildings. As it happened, we had a salamander visiting, as well as an undine. Without both of their help, this man would never have been caught. The danger for Anahita, the undine, really came from the toxin used by Lyssa. Are you familiar with Lyssa?"

Hedy still felt strange naming the woman who had caused so much destruction as the goddess of madness and rage, but Lyssa left both in her wake.

"We are familiar with Lyssa. For all her bluster, she is a minor demigoddess at best. She relies on humans to carry out her plans and that inevitably leads to failure. We are not as concerned about her as we are about a waystation that may leave our travelers in danger. Although, I understand that you destroyed her?" Raluca's question sounded more like a statement of fact, and Hedy wasn't so sure that was the case.

"We don't really know what happened to Lyssa. She hasn't been seen since the night in the cabin when I stabbed her with the knife, but I can't say for certain that she is gone. As much as I hope that she is." Hedy took another sip of her tea and she felt those black eyes scrutinizing her every move.

"And how did you happen to have a weapon in your possession that could inflict damage on a demigod? Not exactly a standard item for a bakery, no?" Raluca gave a dismissive wave of her hand to the room at large.

"I have a rather large collection of curiosities, things that I have acquired, and things passed down through my family. The knife is a relic from an ancestor. I didn't know for sure what it would do to someone like Lyssa, though I did hope it would at least be protection."

Raluca slowly picked up her cup and took another tiny sip. "Yes, I know of your heritage, Miss Leckermaul. I actually knew your ancestor, Rusalia. She was a flawed individual, but I did feel sorry for her over the loss of the children. It is also a shame that she has become the basis of that ludicrous Grimm brothers' story about the candy house and the oven."

Hedy couldn't believe she was talking to someone who had met Rusalia. There was so much she wanted to know, but there was no way she could ask Raluca; Hedy was answering the questions today. She waited for Raluca to continue.

"As you said, it was Lyssa who scratched the undine and caused the danger to your guest. Though if you had insisted that she and the salamander left when you notified the Concierge that you could accept no more travelers, they would have been out of harm's way. Why did you not do that? You clearly knew there was danger, or you would not have called the Concierge." Raluca saw a flash of guilt flit across the woman's face.

"I did ask them to leave but they insisted on staying. They were very brave and wanted to help me. I probably should have insisted, but to be honest, I am not sure that would have made a difference. They are both very strong willed and were quite determined to stay. I consider them both my friends." Hedy's cheeks felt hot and even though in her mind she knew both Ana and Bren chose to stay, she still felt a swirl of guilt flushing her face.

"Waystation hosts are not here to make friends, Miss Leckermaul. They are here to serve our travelers and to keep them safe. You failed in that task. Safety for the travelers is the key to the network; it is why no one knows the locations of all the waystations. No one except myself. Secrecy is how we keep them safe. It is only through good fortune that both of them survived their brush with Lyssa and her human helper. It is now my job to determine if you are fit to continue to host a waystation and I will be spending the next few days determining that. I expect your full cooperation." Raluca stood up from her seat to her full four feet and ten inches of height. She was tired from her long journey and she wanted to lie down.

"Of course. I will be happy to help in any way

I can. Let me show you to a room where you may stay while you are here." Hedy said, trying to hide the distress rising in her gut. She reached for Raluca's small valise, but she was waived away. The old woman had strength to carry her own bag. The pair re-entered the hallway and Hedy led Raluca toward the staircase with the wooden thicket gate.

"Spiders, on your Christmas tree. That is something one sees in my country, but I have not seen such a sight outside of the east. Quite unusual." Raluca said no more as they continued up the stairs toward the second floor.

Neither Hedy nor Raluca heard the pocket door slide open in the hallway where Yami had been quietly listening to their conversation. It seemed she now had something quite interesting to report to Lyssa.

# CHAPTER SEVEN

With Raluca in her room and the shop already closed, Hedy packed up the special order that was due for delivery while she fretted. Her interview with Raluca had not gone well. Everything the woman had said was accurate, but it was said in the worst possible light, and now she faced the risk of being closed down. It was too awful to think about.

"She wasn't there, of course it sounds worse now," Hedy muttered as she boxed up the rugelach she had made for a special order. It was Hanukkah and one of the members of the local social club, The Ancient Order of Rhinos, had called her to inquire if she would make four dozen.

Hedy needed to clear her head and the cool air outside seemed very inviting. She debated walking to the A.O.R. lodge; it was near the high school and she knew the way. But in the end, she elected to drive, rather than risk damage to the pastry. She could always stroll around after she dropped off the treats.

With a plan in mind that consisted of running away for a little while, Hedy bundled up and loaded the boxes into the Corvair. Even just pulling out of the driveway felt good, as if all the tension and worry over the inspection could just be left at the curb. She focused on the road and driving the short distance to the social club lodge.

The members of the Ancient Order of Rhinos was a small, albeit rowdy bunch, with a penchant for wearing fez hats around town. Tonight, they were hosting a members' dinner to celebrate all the December holidays, and Hedy's rugelach was on the menu along with plenty of cocktails. The parking lot was full, and Hedy found a spot on the street, requiring her to parallel park, something she hated, but could do, if pressed.

Parked, and with rugelach in hand, she admired the building as she walked to the front door. It was a squat structure with a roof that rose dramatically in the center to a small tower, as if the roof were the shape of rather flattened funnel. It was small but even with its size, the architecture stood out from its neighbors of craftsman style buildings and brick bungalows.

"Chag Sameach. You must be bringing us the rugelach." A plump lady greeted Hedy at the door.

"Happy holidays to you as well. Yes, I have the delivery; four dozen was the order." She followed the woman into the entry, and could smell the delicious scents from the club's kitchen down the hall.

"Excellent. We were glad you were able to make them for us. I could have dusted off my grandmother's recipe but honestly, I'm just not much of a baker. I'd rather leave that to the professionals." The woman smiled and handed Hedy a check, which she accepted with a smile.

"Thank you. I hope you like them. Please call me if you need anything else. And Happy Hanukkah to you." Hedy found herself back out in the cool afternoon air, mission accomplished.

She dreaded going back to the house. She wasn't ready to continue any more conversation with Raluca at the moment, and even the idea of seeing the house lit up from Darro's efforts didn't excite her. Hedy decided a stroll was exactly what she needed to find her peace of mind.

The A.O.R. lodge was at the end of the street and so Hedy left her car there and headed back toward the shops in town. There was no rain and little wind, which meant it was pleasant enough with her coat wrapped around her and the wool hat keeping her ears warm. She walked slowly and without purpose toward the lights in the windows.

As a local merchant, she felt guilty that she didn't spend more time visiting other shops and making herself known in the community. She was always so busy, either with baking or with travelers, that she rarely found the time to just browse and take in the sights. It was something she really enjoyed doing and she made a mental note to make time for it more often. She passed a few shoppers as she neared the first store and they nodded in greeting; people in the northwest weren't quick to speak to strangers.

Hedy popped into the first shop, which was selling small batches of lotions, soaps, and bath salts. This was the kind of store she could get lost in, smelling all the amazing combinations and testing out various lotions. She found herself testing a hand creme of cardamom and fig that it smelled so good that she decided she had to have it. She'd also have to make a tart with a filling inspired by it.

"It's wonderful, isn't it? There is a local crafter in Buckley that makes them for us. She uses her own goat's milk and all the scents are organically produced. The products are currently in BPA-free plastic containers, but she is transitioning to glass, although I suspect that will raise the price a bit." The salesperson seemed quite enamored of the product, cradling a large bottle of bath salts as she spoke. She either was very passionate about bath products or she worked on commission.

"Yes, I really like this one. I'm going to take the hand creme. In fact, I'll take two." She would give one to Mel as a present.

"Excellent. Can I show you anything else? We have some lovely bullet journals that just came in and some hand poured soy wax candles in recycled mason jars from a local crafter who makes his own wicks." The woman's enthusiasm was such that Hedy hated to disappoint her, but she really wasn't in the market for either item, as eclectic as they might be.

"No, I think I am good with just the two lotions but thank you. This is a lovely store. I'll be sure to come by again. Please give my compliments to the owner." Hedy waited at the birch wood counter while the salesperson carefully wrapped each lotion in recycled tissue paper and then placed them in a brown Kraft bag.

"Well, that's me. My name is Kaitlyn. The Owl and Jam Jar is my store." Kaitlyn tied the handles of the bag closed with a bit of twine and placed the bag near Hedy. "That will be forty-two dollars, please."

Hedy gulped slightly; she hadn't looked at the price because she was so enamored with the scent. Apparently, the price for cardamom fig goat's milk creme was quite high, even in BPA-free plastic containers.

"Here you go." She handed cash to Kaitlyn, tallying up that the purchase just about wiped out her rugelach money. Oh well, it was amazing lotion.

"Thank you. I'll slip in a flyer about some events we are hosting in January. We will be having a yarn tasting and a trunk show for the chandler who makes the candles I was telling you about. Of course, we'll be at the Christmas market this weekend as well." Kaitlyn spoke in a clipped tone and she briefly smiled at Hedy as she handed her the change. Hedy wondered if the pretty Korean-American woman was even thirty years old; she seemed young to own a shop of her own.

"I will be there as well. I run the bakery on Griffin, the Gingerbread Hag. Perhaps I'll see you there." Hedy took the purchase and also one of Kaitlyn's cards; they were actually printed on a thin slice of wood.

"Enjoy your purchase." Kaitlyn's voice followed Hedy out the front door of the shop.

Next door was the shop that Mel had told her about, the Red Bat. Hedy was immediately struck by the window display. The mannequin was wearing a jeweled red circle skirt with a full white crinoline and a gorgeous green angora sweater. It looked like something right out of a Christmas sock hop in the 1950s and Hedy thought it looked wonderful. There were various retro toys displayed at its feet and a large cut out of mistletoe, also covered in sparkles, hanging from the ceiling.

"My kind of shop," Hedy breathed, excited to see what kind of wares the owner might have inside.

"Good afternoon, Miss. Welcome to the Red Bat." The man behind the counter was arranging gloves in a rainbow pattern onto a large platter, but clearly his eye was on the door.

"Good afternoon. You have a lovely shop." Hedy only needed a moment to make that statement; the shop wasn't like a typical thrift shop, with everything hodge-podge and smelling slightly musty. The Red Bat had things organized by era, by color, and then by size. It was an organizational dream for someone like Hedy.

"Well thank you, Miss. I do try. What brings you in today?" The man's voice was pleasant with a touch of gravel to it along with a slight accent that Hedy couldn't place. Hedy detected none of the fake welcoming tone that could be found when shopping. He left his rainbow display and came around the counter, looking very dapper in a pair of pinstripe pants and a Christmas pattern vest.

"I am just browsing. A friend mentioned your shop and she knows my penchant for vintage clothing, so I thought I would stop in. My name is Hedy, by the way." She felt a little foolish introducing herself, but the man seemed quite friendly.

"Pleased to meet you, Hedy. My name is Michael, proprietor of The Red Bat. I hope you don't mind me saying that you have a rather impressive hairstyle. A beehive is one of my favorites." Michael was moving closer to Hedy, adjusting hangers as he went for imperceptible flaws. Hedy felt her cheeks blush. With his curly, dark hair and blue eyes, he looked quite debonair.

"Well, thank you, Michael. I am a fan of an earlier era and I do like a bit of fun. I thought I would see what you might have that would be appropriate for the Christmas market on Saturday; I'll be tending a booth there." Hedy began to follow him as he made his way over toward the clothing under the neon "60s" sign.

"Oh, a fellow vendor. I'll be there as well, bringing a small sampling in hopes of luring suburbanites out of the chain stores and their Ugg boots. What will you be selling?" Michael was pulling items from the rack, hanging each sideways on a bar so that Hedy could see the selections. Without even asking, he had her size.

"I own the bakery on Griffin Avenue, The Gingerbread Hag. I'll be there selling my Krampus cookies." Hedy's eye was immediately drawn to a gorgeous, red dotted swiss swing dress with sheer sleeves and a high ruffled collar.

"I have heard great things about that shop. My apologies for not coming to visit. Since I opened, I've hardly had a moment that wasn't occupied with getting the shop in the best shape possible. The previous store in this space was a barber shop and I am still finding little pockets of hair in the strangest places." Michael's curls shook as he laughed, which made it seem all the more amusing.

"Well, I hope you will come by the shop sometime or visit me at the Market if you have a moment. I'll even give you a cookie." Hedy smiled at him, and to her surprise, she really was hoping to see him again soon. There was something quite interesting about him, with his dark blue eyes that had more than a glint of mischief.

"Well, would you like to try any of these beauties on to see what suits you? Personally, I could see you in any of them, but I see you have your eye on the dotted swiss. It's reminiscent of a Mary Quant design but without the designer price tag, naturally."

Michael picked up the dress and held it up toward Hedy, careful not to actually invade her space. There was a line between helpful and intrusive and he seemed well aware of it. A man selling women's clothing had to be respectful.

"Yes, I love it and I think it will just fit, especially since it is more of an A line shape. That's a style that is quite forgiving of my love of cookies." Hedy held the dress closer and took a look in the mirror; it was exactly the style she would have chosen for herself.

"Wonderful. I have some adorable flats if you need them or perhaps a red pocketbook. I suspect though that you have a full wardrobe of accessories." Michael laughed again and Hedy nodded; yes, she had more than her share of accessories gathered throughout her travels.

"Well, let's ring you up then so you can be back to tending your bakery. I can't wait to see you debut this dress at the Christmas market."

Michael led the way to the front counter and Hedy placed the dress on the black Formica countertop. Her troubles were still waiting for her back at the shop, but she felt lighter having been out in the world and meeting what she hoped was a new friend. A handsome new friend.

"Thank you so much for the dress. I can see myself coming back again soon for more treasures. And do come by the shop, I'd love to show you around." Hedy fished a business card out of her purse as she gathered her wallet to pay. It wasn't fancy like Kaitlyn's wooden cards, but it was rather elegant, if Hedy said so herself.

"I will come by at my first opportunity. Thank you for the invitation, and thank you for the purchase. I'll see you on Saturday, Hedy." Michael carefully folded the dress and placed it in a black bag with red tissue paper. Hedy noticed the small bat printed on the top of the receipt.

"Thank you, Michael. See you then." Hedy waved as she left the shop, watching him return to his rainbow glove display. The Christmas market was only two days away and she was now looking forward to it. She smiled as she walked back toward the Corvair and the return trip to the shop.

# CHAPTER EIGHT

Mel was really in the Christmas spirit this year. Maybe it was working all day with gingerbread and the fact that she had someone now to kiss under the mistletoe, but she was really feeling festive. The annual trip out to the Christmas tree farm seemed like an especially good idea, even piled in the family Jeep with her mom and her brother. She sent Ana a text with a kiss emoji next to a crashing wave before sticking her phone in her pocket. Cell service out at the tree arm would be spotty.

"Who is ready for some Christmas carols?" Mel's mother, Candace, was fiddling with the satellite radio instead of keeping her eyes on the road.

"Hey, Mom, let me do that. You drive, okay?" Mel had called shotgun before they left the house and her brother, Mark, was in the backseat.

"No Christmas songs, okay? Jeez, I hate that stuff," Mark whined from his seat and Mel looked for the "Holly" station on the dial. The Waitresses' Christmas Wrapping filled the car. "Ah crap," said Mark.

"That's enough, Mark. 'Tis the season, you know. You gotta get in the mood for the tree farm. Uncle Jim and Dylan will be there. I don't know if Jim is bringing his girlfriend or not." Candace said the word "girlfriend" with a bit too much emphasis. Clearly, she was not a fan.

"Fine, but I am not going on any hayride. I'm telling you that right now." Mark sulked in the seat, more annoyed than anything that his cellphone had no range out near the tree farm.

They pulled into the driveway marked with a large tree cut out painted with reflective paint and found a spot in the rather muddy field that served for parking. Apparently, half of Enumclaw must have decided that tonight was a good night to get a tree because the lot was packed.

"Wow, what's with tonight? It's not even the weekend," Mel asked no one in particular but her mother answered.

"I think tonight is the Boy Scout event out here. They are doing some kind of fundraiser. Plus, I think the chamber choir is also here to perform. Anyway, grab the work gloves in the back, Mark."

He grunted in reply and they all gingerly stepped out of the Jeep, trying to avoid mud. Mel had wisely worn some rubber boots, but Mark was still in his old Converse and she could hear them squish. It made her laugh.

"Let's find our tree." Candace headed toward the strings of lights that framed the barn. It wouldn't be too much longer before it was really dark, and the bonfire was lit. Mel always enjoyed the bonfire.

Jim and Dylan were waiting near the entrance, with no sight of the girlfriend; it was just the two of them. Dylan, twelve years old and shy by nature, gave a short wave toward them. Mel thought he looked like a miniature version of Mark, which wasn't necessarily a compliment. The kid had dark hair and a rather underdeveloped chin. Hopefully he'd grow a beard when he grew up, though Mark hadn't taken the hint yet.

"Hi, you guys. Good to see you." Mel reached out and gave Dylan's hair a tussle. He smiled at her in return. Candace gave Jim a hug; they had been close as siblings since their parents had died years ago. Now, both divorced and raising kids, they had even more in common.

"Ready for some cider, Dylan?" Candace asked the boy and he nodded quickly. "Well, lead the way. Let's get inside." The group entered the lot and headed back toward the barn where there was cider and donuts for sale. Mel could see that a line was forming. There was a troop of Cub Scouts in full uniform scampering about, all clambering for a glass; this could take a while.

"Jim and I can wait in line for the cider if you guys want to start looking around." Candace said. Mel figured Mom wanted a chance to grill Uncle Jim about his girlfriend in private.

"Yeah, we can do that." Mel and Dylan peeled off from the group, with Mark hovering beyond them somewhere.

A boy about Dylan's age came running up, cheeks bright red from the run. "Hey, Dylan. Wanna see something cool? We found something." Mel was pleased to see Dylan had a friend; she wasn't so sure he was a popular kid at school, being so shy.

"Yeah, but I have to ask my Dad." Dylan slipped back toward the line and in a few seconds was back. "He said I could go but I have to stay nearby. Is it far?"

"Nah, it's close. Come on." The kid turned and began running back the way he came, with Dylan hot on his heels. He turned back and gave Mel a wave.

"Have fun," she called out and she headed over toward the makeshift stage to watch the singers lineup. Tonight would be fun.

* * *

"We gotta go through the fence here." Randy was leading Dylan to the very edge of the farm property, which butted up to the forest and Mount Enumclaw. The darkness was getting thicker and the Christmas tree lights weren't helping.

"This is pretty far, Randy. I don't think my dad would want me to leave the farm." Dylan was hesitating at the fence, while Randy squeezed through the opening.

"Oh, come on. It's just over here, hardly passed

the fence. We found this cool cave entrance. The guys have flashlights. We think it is part of an old mine tunnel. You gotta see it." Randy had befriended Dylan part way through the school year and Dylan didn't relish the prospect of disappointing his friend. He didn't have enough to risk the loss.

"Okay. If it is just on the edge here, I suppose that's okay." Dylan slipped through the fence easily and followed Randy's red jacket toward the dark of the forest. He did not like this, but he couldn't look afraid.

As they entered the forest, Dylan was worried he was going to trip in the darkness. There was a path of sorts and he kept his eyes fixed on the red of Randy's jacket. Ahead, he saw the faint glow of light from behind a rock.

"That's it. The entrance to the cave. See, it isn't far." Randy's voice sounded thin in the echo of the trees. Dylan would be glad to get to the light and then make his way back to the farm.

"Randy, is that you?" Dylan heard the voice of Tamara, another classmate, from behind the rock. Dylan had a crush on Tamara and had since last year. Every time he saw her, he felt that slightly sickening feeling in his stomach. Now he definitely needed to keep cool.

"Yeah, and I brought Dylan. You guys find anything?" Randy rounded the edge of the rock and the light from the flashlights was coming from deeper into the cave. Tamara was standing near the entrance, holding a small flashlight.

"Steve and Harley are down there. I waited here for you. Hi, Dylan." Tamara gave him a quick nod and Dylan nodded in return. It was the most she had said to him in months.

"Well, let's go. I bet there is something cool down there. Maybe even gold." Randy charged ahead, leaving Tamara and Dylan to bring up the rear. The light seemed deep inside the cave, but at least they had the small light from Tamara's flashlight to guide them into the dark.

Randy called out to Steve and Harley, but no one responded. "How deep did they go? Dang, you think they can't hear me?" Randy hollered again and this time, they heard a voice, very faint, calling back. They still hadn't reached the orangish light.

"Maybe we should head back up. We can tell Steve and Harley to come back. I'm not sure I want to be this far down in here," Tamara said, giving voice to what Dylan had been thinking and he immediately began nodding in the darkness.

"Yeah, Randy. I should be getting back. My dad is going to start looking for me." Dylan saw Randy's red coat pause ahead of them.

"Well, yeah, maybe. We can come back in the daylight with more lights." Randy paused and cleared his throat to holler again. "Hey, Steve, Harley, come on back. Come back, you guys." The sound bounced around the cave walls and buffeted their ears.

In the darkness they heard a small voice calling back to them. “Come here. We need help.”

“Oh, crap. Maybe they are stuck. We gotta go down and get them.” Randy started walking again, following the glow of Tamara’s flashlight.

“Maybe we should get help first?” Tamara sounded scared to Dylan and his own prickles on the back of his neck were saying the same thing. This seemed like a bad idea.

“No, we gotta help them. They can’t be much further, see the light is getting brighter,” Randy insisted. He was right, the light was getting stronger, but it had a weird reddish orange tint to it.

They followed the tunnel down, getting closer and closer to the light, and the sounds of the boys’ cries for help.

# CHAPTER NINE

Hedy was on Dumaine Street, between Royal and Chartres, a stretch that she had walked a hundred times. She could find her way to Delphine and Tante's shop in the French Quarter with her eyes closed. It was just past the Cornstalk Hotel and far enough away from trashy Bourbon Street that the stench of stale booze and piss was out of the spring breeze.

She loved this part of the Quarter, with cobbled streets and iron balconies draped with riotous flowers and a few errant Mardi-Gras beads. But now, the door to Delphine's psychic shop was locked and she was frantically twisting the old knob; it had never been locked to her before.

"She ain't there, Chère. You won't find her." An old woman was sitting on a small wooden bench along the wall next to the shop. She smelled like chicory.

"Where is she? She's always here in the evening. I need to find Delphine." She heard her own voice, younger and urgent; the sound of another life from another time. Where was Delphine? What had Anita done to her? There was sweat pooling in the small of her back, clammy in the night breeze. Her breath was shallow and tight in her chest.

"She ain't there, Chère. You won't find her." The old woman was gone and, in her place, sat a large fox, brushing its tail with its paw, its lips cracked in a sly smile. The teeth were glinting under the lamp light.

She continued on down Dumaine but it wasn't the Dumaine Street she knew. Instead of the shops selling Cajun art, the museum of Voodoo, and the po'boy restaurant, there were just rows and rows of shotgun houses, painted in easter egg shades of yellow, blue, and purple. Row after row of the narrow houses, with wooden slat doors and small front windows. Everything seemed wrong.

"Delphine? Where are you? I need your help. Delphine!" she called but no one answered. Zydeco music was playing from one of the houses and someone had a pot of gumbo cooking; she could smell the filé powder and the green peppers, slowly decomposing into something thick and inseparable. She heard the call of the red-winged blackbird, telling on her.

She was running out of time. She had no more breath in her lungs and the air around her felt solid, far too thick to gulp.

"Delphine! Help me! Anita's done a terrible thing. We have to help Julius." Her voice sounded far away, like it was being sucked into a doorway and pulled out of the night air. She knew Delphine would never hear her. She would have to find Julius on her own. No one was listening, no one was there. Sweat trickled into her eyes.

"Who is Delphine, Chère? You can tell me." The fox was walking beside her and no matter how quickly she walked, it easily loped alongside, keeping pace.

"Delphine is my friend. She is Julius' friend. I need her." Hedy didn't have time for these questions.

The fox seemed very interested and was listening intently to her answer.

"And who is Julius? You can tell me." The fox had stopped and now she was in St. Louis Cemetery No. 1, surrounded by the above-ground stone tombs of New Orleans that had marked time for the last four hundred years.

"No, not here. We can't be here. Not at night. I have to go find Julius." She started to run but her feet were bolted to the crushed rock and compact dirt. The fox was watching her quizzically.

"Forget about Julius. Forget about Delphine. Forget about this place. This is your past; I want to know about the present. Who are you?" the fox pressed, growing impatient.

"I can't forget, don't you understand? They need me, someone needs me. Someone is looking for me. I am needed."

The fox would never understand her, that much was clear.

"Tell me what I want to know." The fox began to snarl, fangs growing longer and claws sharpening. She couldn't move at all and she couldn't scream. The fox was coming closer to her but now it was the silhouette of darkness, faceless and menacing, swallowing up the stone tombs one by one.

"Hedy, hear me. Hedy, wake up. Dreams, only dreams." The voice called to her, as if from above, as if coming from a bluish white light that was blanketing her. It was familiar and friendly and calling her, pulling on her mind. She heard the fox shadow hiss and then withdraw, leaving her alone in the cemetery.

"Wake. Wake up." The voice of Adelaide pulled at her, drawing her mind out of the dark swirl of memories. She woke with a start, sitting up in her bed with sweat soaking her cotton nightgown and the flutter of her curtains moving the cold air.

"Adelaide? Was that you?" Hedy's voice was shaky. She hadn't dreamed about New Orleans in a long time, but this dream seemed different somehow. Someone was questioning her, chasing her, probing her mind. She couldn't remember who.

The room was quiet. The curtains had stopped fluttering, but Hedy wished Adelaide would appear and help her remember. Was it an animal in the dream? It was an old woman. Hedy pictured the face again, and then watched it morph into the figure of a fox.

"Yes, a fox. It was a fox, Adelaide," she called out but Adelaide didn't answer. The room was still dark and there were hours left until daybreak, but Hedy didn't dare close her eyes.

She was sure the fox would be waiting in her dream if she did.

# CHAPTER TEN

Friday dawned and Hedy was up to watch it, unable to stay in bed any longer. Neither of her guests had appeared for dinner the night before, so she found herself in her room early with nothing but her thoughts and fragments of bad dreams. She had left a tray outside each of their rooms, but both were untouched.

"You're up early, Hedy. I was about to head out for my morning flight." Alice was preening her feathers and seemed delighted that someone was up so early to talk with her. Zelda and Maurice were nowhere to be seen.

"Yes, I couldn't sleep. It's a bit stressful right now and my mind is going a million miles a second, hibbity-jibbity. I had a terrible dream and it seemed like a good idea to get up and work instead of tossing in bed." Alice nodded as if she understood what Hedy was saying but in truth, her bird brain never had multiple thoughts at once.

"Haven't seen much of your guests. Not to be rude, but I liked the other two better," Alice chirped in a gossip like fashion and finished her feather fluffing. Time to get to the sky.

"Well, it would be rude of me to comment but I did enjoy Bren and Ana. In fact, I hope to see Ana this weekend at the market. It's been awhile."

"Well, I must dash now. I'll catch some breakfast outside, so don't worry about me. Ta-Ta." Alice trilled and left her perch, heading for the small window over the sink that Hedy always kept open for her. In a flash, the magpie was gone, and Hedy was alone again.

"Mel won't be here for hours. Perhaps I could read for a bit." Hedy liked the sound of her voice in the empty kitchen; it made her feel less edgy.

She poured herself a cup of coffee from the percolator she had on the stove. She took her cup and headed into the entry, stopping to admire the tree as she went. It really was a beautiful tree, with all the spiders and soft silver lights. Whether it was traditional or not was a matter of interpretation, but it was nonetheless a lovely thing.

On a small roll-top desk against the wall, Hedy found the book she was looking for. "Encyclopedia of World Mythology," Hedy read the title aloud and smiled. The author might be shocked at how many of the entries in the book she had hosted in her waystation. Hedy took the book and her coffee into the little parlor near the front door and settled into an overstuffed velvet chair, wrapping a wool throw around her. This early in the morning, the house was chilly.

"Let's see what we can learn." Hedy opened the

cover and gazed across the Table of Contents. The entries were grouped by region. Hedy was well familiar with European legends, Russian legends, Mediterranean legends, and even some of those from the Americas. She needed to learn more about Africa and Asia.

Hedy skimmed the pages for Asia, taking in briefly information about Jiangshi, vampires from China, and Dokkaebi, Korean goblins. It wasn't that she didn't find them interesting, but her mind was having a hard time settling down to the task of actually reading. She was tired but there would be no way she would be sleeping for a while. Her eyes flitted over the entry for Kitsune from Japan and she stopped.

"What's this? 'A kitsune is a Japanese fox spirit, a being that can shapeshift into various human forms once it reaches one hundred years of age. Kitsune can be kind and benevolent but are most often mischievous and prone to trickery. In their fox form, kitsune have nine tails and can insert themselves into the dreams of humans.'"

Hedy read the passage again, this time silently, and then stared off toward the light in the window. Foxes. First, the fox attacks on the local farms, then this morning's nightmare with the fox. Now the entry about kitsune. Why so many references to foxes? It seemed a strange coincidence for sure, and she was never one for coincidences. Was it possible that Yami was a kitsune and she had infiltrated Hedy's dreams? Why would she want to do that?

"Here you are. I thought I heard something in here." Maurice had found his way to the parlor, still looking sleepy. He hopped up to the arm of the chair and found a spot in the wool throw.

"Yes, just doing a bit of reading. About Japanese fox spirits actually." Hedy felt him give a shudder.

"Foxes are worthless creatures. Alice told me about the attacks on the farms around here and I say good riddance to the whole skulk of foxes responsible." Hedy knew very well that Maurice had a tragic history involving foxes; they had slaughtered his family.

"Have you ever heard of a kitsune, Maurice? A fox spirit that can shapeshift into human form?" Maurice wasn't prone to reading anything that wasn't philosophical in nature, but in his early years, he had traveled with a necromancer who frequented the dark edges of polite society. Perhaps Maurice had encountered one.

"Ugh, no, thank goodness. At least, not to my knowledge. But if they can shapeshift, how would you know? As awful as traveling with Dr. Zee was, and it was awful, he at least had the decency to keep me clear of any shapeshifters. No one can trust them." As curious as Hedy was to know about Maurice's time on the road, she never pried because she knew those days held sad memories for him.

"Oh, not all shapeshifters, Maurice. I knew a very nice one in Louisiana; his name is Louis. Anyway, this entry caught my eye. Seems like foxes have been a topic of discussion lately so that is probably why. And perhaps don't wish too hard for the local foxes to be harmed. Remember our friend, Ren? We wouldn't want anything to happen to him." She heard Maurice sniff loudly, signaling his disagreement, but he said nothing.

"How about some breakfast? I could do with a bite." Maurice jumped lightly from the chair and began padding his way toward the kitchen. Hedy closed the book and unwrapped from the throw. She wondered if she would see either of her guests anytime soon.

"Right behind you, Maurice," Hedy called after the chinchilla as she placed the book back on the roll-top desk. She had such a feeling of unease and she just couldn't shake it. she hated to suspect her guest of being behind her dream but the thought bored itself into her brain and would not come out.

* * *

Maurice had eaten his kippers and gone off to do something taxing, like taking a nap, when Raluca appeared. Hedy was washing dishes and had her back to the doorway, but she could just feel someone was there. If there had been a rustling sound, she would have thought it was Adelaide. Hedy turned slowly to see the small woman standing there, watching.

"Oh, good morning, I didn't hear you come down the stairs. I hope you slept well." Hedy tried to smile her very best welcome smile, but she feared it looked more like a grimace today.

"I have a very light step. I would have been amazed if you had heard me." Raluca was dressed in periwinkle blue today, another meticulous Chanel suit. The pearls around her neck could probably keep the bakery running for several years.

"Can I make you some breakfast? Coffee, perhaps?" Raluca stayed where she was in the doorway and gave the kitchen a skeptical look, though it was spotless.

"You Americans drink far too much coffee. No wonder you are so jittery all the time. A cup of tea would be fine and a piece of dry toast. I will take it in the cafe area." With that, Raluca left the kitchen. There was not a sound on the creaky wooden floors.

Toast and tea in hand, Hedy dreaded going into the shop, which was abnormal. She loved it there, with the scent of spices and warmth and treats waiting for someone to delight in them. It was an uncomfortable feeling to be heading into *her* shop and feel dread.

"Here we are." Hedy brought the breakfast to the table Raluca had chosen, which was as far from the window as she could get.

"Where is your traveler? I have not met her yet. Yami Hayashi, is it not?" No surprise that Raluca knew the name of Hedy's traveler. She likely knew the guests of every waystation on the west coast.

"She is not an early riser. In fact, I did not see her last night after your arrival. She must have business she is attending to." It was rare to have a traveler disappear; Enumclaw did not have a large number of sights that would keep someone away for that long.

"I must speak with her before I can conclude my investigation. I have been attempting to reach Mr. Aldebrand, but he has not been responsive to my inquiries," Raluca said flatly as she poured herself a cup of tea from the small pot before her. She gave it a sniff and found it adequate.

"He was traveling to New York, but I would assume he is there by now. He has been gone two weeks." Hedy felt the words die in her mouth as Raluca gave her a look that said she spoke the obvious.

"Yes, I am aware of his plans. I have his waystation reports all the way from here to New York. Once he arrived though, he disappeared." Raluca took a small nibble on her wheat toast and returned to her tea.

"I wish I could be of help to you, but I don't have a way to reach him. I do know the whereabouts of Anahita Sohrab, if you would like to speak to her." Hedy again saw the look from Raluca that she was stating something obvious.

"I know where she is. It has been arranged that she will meet me here tomorrow."

"Well, you have everything in hand, then. I can go about my business in the meantime, yes?" Hedy felt her patience slipping and she hoped it wasn't clear to Raluca, though there wasn't likely much that she missed.

"Behave as normal, please. I wish to see you at your ease." Raluca smiled and there was nothing warm or easy in that look. Hedy gave her a short nod and turned back to the counter to begin making her snail cinnamon rolls. Before Hedy could think of something to say to fill the silence, there was a pounding on the front door.

Hedy hurried over and saw Mel through the glass, looking anxious. Hedy unlocked the door and ushered her inside.

"Mel, what is happening? You look upset." She brought Mel into the shop and saw the girl pause at the sight of Raluca. She had not been there for the Moroaica's arrival. "Mel, this is my guest, Raluca Vaduva. Mel is a student in town that helps me in the shop."

Raluca gave Mel a slight nod before returning to her toast.

"Hedy, something happened last night, at the tree farm. Something with my cousin, Dylan, and his friends." Mel was speaking too quickly, and Hedy needed her to calm down.

"Mel, sit and let me get you a cup of tea. Tell me slowly what happened."

Mel paused before continuing. "Dylan and his friends left the farm and went into the forest, into a cave. When they didn't come back, we went looking for them. Luckily, the cave wasn't that far from the farm. We were calling to them and they must have heard our voices, because they were just coming out of the cave when we got there." Mel took a sip of the tea that Hedy brought her.

"Was anyone hurt?" Hedy watched Mel as she shook her head slightly.

"That's just it. No one is hurt physically. They didn't even have a scratch on them. But there is something wrong. I could tell as soon as they followed us out of the woods."

"What do you mean?" Hedy sat down at Mel's table to watch the girl's face.

"At first, I thought it was just shock, you know, from having a close call in the woods. Maybe they thought they were going to get into big trouble, and there was definitely a risk for that; my Uncle Jim was furious. But everyone was just glad to have them back safely. But walking back from the woods, I watched them, and they were communicating without speaking." Mel looked at Hedy with a lost look, like she couldn't explain what she had seen.

"Okay, take it slowly. What did they do?"

"One of the kids, I think his name was Harley, seemed like the ringleader. They had all been walking separately, near their parents, when all of a sudden and without a word, they all paused and grouped around Harley, walking together in a cluster. They walked like that for a few moments, as close as they could be without tripping over each other, and then again, without a word, the group broke up. Dylan and some girl paired off and walked near the edge of us. Again, none of them said anything. By then, we were back at the tree farm and people were coming up to see if they were alright. I watched them all look to Harley, who said nothing, but then they would answer the questions, using just a few words. It was the weirdest thing." Mel took another sip of tea, clearly remembering the scene as she spoke.

"The adults were all so relieved that they weren't watching them that closely when we got back but I saw this kid, Randy, who is my cousin's friend, kick his own dog to get it out of the way. And Dylan laughed when he saw it. That's not Dylan's way. He is the sweetest kid. He would never laugh at that." Mel started to cry, wiping the tears furiously with her sleeve.

"Okay, let's be calm about this. The kids probably were scared to death and afraid of getting in trouble about it. No doubt that contributed to them acting tough and rough when they got back. I would say your family should just keep an eye on Dylan and I bet he returns to his old self in a day or two. Stuck in a dark cave, I might lash out, too." Hedy gave Mel's arm a pat and hoped she had reassured her. It was strange, certainly, but a good scare could make people act strangely.

"I hope you are right. I probably won't see him again until the Christmas market, but I'll be watching him to see if he is still acting weird. Oh, and speaking of weird, the fox attacks seem to have gotten worse. Even with all the trapping."

Mel took another sip and Hedy waited for her to continue.

"Last night, a fox took down several goats at some farm in Buckley, where they make soap and lotions. How could a fox take on something that big?" Mel and Hedy both saw Raluca turn toward them for the first time.

"Fox attacks, you say? Quite unusual. Tell me about it." The old woman's face was pinched in what Hedy guessed was anticipation.

Hedy spoke up. "We've had some fox attacks on poultry this week, small creatures mainly. The farmers have been setting traps aggressively, which we have been worried about as we have reason to think it may not be a local fox causing the damage. But now taking down goats? It really seems unlikely it is a fox," Hedy said. She wasn't quite prepared to tell Raluca about Ren and his request for assistance.

"What makes everyone think it is a fox? Has the creature been seen?" Raluca spoke slowly, digesting the information as she went.

"My uncle said it was the claw and bite marks, and some reddish fur on the bodies. No one has seen the actual fox or foxes at work." Mel spoke quietly, clearly intimidated by the old woman.

Raluca smiled with a toothy grin. "Don't worry, child. I won't bite like this phantom fox. You need not be afraid of me. But I may have some ideas about these attacks." She said no more, returning to her tea. Mel and Hedy exchanged puzzled looks but Hedy tried to brush it off.

"Let's get the shop ready to open and later, you can call your uncle to check on Dylan. I'll bet he is better already." Hedy rose from the table and went back to her dough. It wasn't even nine in the morning and already the day had taken a very strange turn.

# CHAPTER ELEVEN

Mid-morning found Hedy upstairs in the library looking for Adelaide.

"Adelaide, I am really shook up and I could use your help. You saved me from the dream. Can you tell me anything that would help understand who was after me?" She knew she was likely wasting her time - the ghost only chimed in when she felt like it - but Adelaide had come through when it really counted. Adelaide's information had saved Anahita from Lyssa. Maybe she would do the same now.

Hedy waited but there wasn't a sound other than the slight hiss and flicker of the candle. Her mind tried to plan a way to reach Adelaide but the only idea she had was too dangerous. As scary as her nightmare had been, she wasn't sure she could dare risk trying a spirit board to reach the hiding ghost. Who knew what malevolent being might tag along, finding an easy portal into the house. That was the last thing they needed.

"I need someone who communes with spirits

and who can make contact, keeping the dangerous spirits away. I need the coven." Hedy didn't realize she was speaking out loud but the sound of her voice bounced back against the library walls. If Adelaide had any thoughts to contribute, she didn't pipe up.

"I'll call Helen." Hedy brought the candle out of the room, blowing carefully to avoid splattering the wall with wax. She left the taper on the table near the library door and hurried downstairs, almost tripping on the berry bramble gate as she went.

"What's happening? What's the rush?" Mel chimed in from the counter as Hedy steamed passed the open doorway in the kitchen.

"I'm calling Helen with the coven. I need a connection to Adelaide." Hedy flipped through her paper Rolodex until she located the new card with the 'Sisters of the Crescent Moon Coven' scrawled across the top. Helen was their leader. She had met the group a few months back when they had held a seance to meet Adelaide.

Hedy didn't wait for Mel to ask any more questions. She picked up the receiver to the land line and dialed the witch.

"Hello?" The voice on the end of the line sounded tense, which Hedy found was typical for Helen. Apparently being a witch did not make someone mellow.

"Hi, Helen. It's Hedy Leckermaul at the bakery. I was hoping I could trouble you for a house call."

Hedy's voice had its own edge of tension, though she was trying very hard to sound chipper.

"House call? I'm not sure I understand..." Helen faltered.

"A witch house call, if that makes sense. I need help reaching Adelaide. It's rather urgent." Hedy hoped Helen wouldn't say no; otherwise she might be forced to try it on her own and that was a risky option. The high witch however did not disappoint.

"I would be delighted to try to reach your spirit. Last time, we assembled the whole coven. What did you have in mind?"

"I need some specific answers and Adelaide tends to speak in riddles. I thought perhaps using a spirit board..." Hedy paused and the line was quiet.

"Hedy...I don't know. Spirit boards are dangerous. Think of them like open windows. Any spirit can crawl in when you have them open. Are you sure?" To Helen's credit, at least she didn't say no outright.

"I know the risk, but I thought perhaps if you did a grounding spell of some kind, we could minimize the risk. You'd know better than me, of course." Hedy chewed on a ragged spot on her otherwise filed nails. She needed the witch's help and telling her how to conduct her rituals likely wasn't going to get it.

"Well, alright. We could try. When do you want to do this?"

"How about now?"

* * *

Forty-five minutes later, a rather disheveled witch walked through Hedy's front door. "Helen, thank you for coming over. I really do appreciate it."

"Well, you did say it was urgent. You were kind enough to host the coven so it is the least I can do to return the favor. Where shall we set up?" Helen was remarkable in her unremarkableness and Hedy envied her. Hedy's hair and style made her stand out wherever she went but Helen could have blended into wall paper. She had hair that might be called blonde, if someone was being charitable, and an average frame, average height, and average face. Nothing stood out about Helen. If she hadn't been dressed in all black, with the silver pentacle hanging onto her average bosom, she could have been inserted into any scene in any movie where the cast called for Extra No 2.

"If you will follow me, I think the library upstairs would be best. That is Adelaide's favorite room." Hedy led the way passed the Christmas tree, pushing aside the wooden bramble gate. She gazed over her shoulder to make sure Helen was still with her. The woman was paused, staring at the brown shingle in the box that hung on Hedy's wall.

"What is that, if I may ask? It gives off this aura

that is so strong I can practically taste it. It must have belonged to a powerful witch once." Helen held her fingers just above the glass that separated the ancient shingle from the roof of the Gingerbread Hag of legend.

"My ancestor was the witch from Hansel and Gretel. I'll gladly tell you the story sometime over a pot of tea. Perhaps after we are done." Hedy hoped she hadn't been too obvious in her desire to keep things moving toward the library. With a slight nod, Helen followed Hedy's steps up the carpeted stairs.

Hedy pulled the matches from her apron pocket and lit the pillar again. The wax had barely hardened. Pressing open the door, she used the pillar to light several smaller candles that rested on shelves throughout the library. The room had a soft glow of candlelight.

"Please, have a seat at the table." Hedy gestured toward the tiny table she had in the center of the room.

"First, I must prepare the space. I must open a circle around the table, greet the four cardinal points and then close the circle with us inside. It will keep whatever might come through the board from getting loose. At least I hope it will." Helen's tight voice sounded unsure. So much for Hedy's plan of bringing in an expert.

Helen opened up her black canvas tote bag and drew out the large mason jar of rock salt. She placed a spirit board on the table, along with a wooden planchette, and three red votive candles. Helen's movements were brisk and efficient. She may have had her doubts, but the witch was going about it all with high energy.

"Hedy, have a seat at the table. I will open the circle and invoke the cardinal points. You should work on keeping your mind clear. Try not to think about Adelaide or your concerns. Think pleasant thoughts. We want the atmosphere to be charged with neutral or positive energy. Nothing negative." Helen's words were clipped as she twisted the lid off the mason jar.

With her eyes closed, Hedy tried thinking about spices she wanted to order for the shop - keeping her thoughts light and easy. As much as she tried to focus on cinnamon from Sri Lanka and the high price of saffron, her thoughts kept going back to the dream and the terror of being chased. Keeping light thoughts was a much harder task than she would have thought.

She squinted her eyes hard, willing away the images and she let her mind drift, away from spices. The face of Michael floated across her eyes. He had such nice curly hair - a beautiful, soft black. His eyes had a marvelous little crinkle at each corner and they were a brilliant shade of deep blue, with the slightest flecks of gold. The corners of his mouth seemed to be always ready to smile and even the slight stubble on his chin looked like it would be soft to the touch.

"Hedy...Hedy. Focus now." Helen's tight voice

snatched the image of Michael from her vision and her eyes flicked open. She felt the warmth in her cheeks from blushing. Could the witch see it?

"I'm ready." Hedy watched Helen sit across the table from her. There was a tight circle of salt on the floor around them. The three candles were lit and placed on three sides of the board.

"We will start with just me using the planchette. If we have trouble connecting with Adelaide, I may ask you to join me, but I find the signal is usually clearer if one person is connected to the board." Helen's fingers were already lightly touching the heart shaped planchette. Hedy wondered briefly if what Helen said was true or if it was because Helen liked being in charge. She pushed the thought quickly away; no negative thoughts were allowed.

"Dear Adelaide. We call you to help us. Our friend, Hedy, has questions and she needs your help. Adelaide, we call you to us, into this sacred space."

Helen's voice was still tight but now it had a ring of the theatrics that Hedy had remembered from the first meeting. Perhaps this was her witch stage voice.

"Hedy, speak your question. What do you wish to know?" Helen stage whispered to her, as if Adelaide couldn't hear everything they said.

"Adelaide. Thank you for saving me from that nightmare. You pulled me from the dream. But what was chasing me? Who was in the dream asking me questions?" Hedy spoke in measured tones, pausing between each word slightly. She had no idea why she did this but it seemed appropriate. Perhaps it took longer to reach the spirit realm than just speaking into the air.

The planchette began to move, crawling across the board and finding a strange swiveling pattern across the edges, not landing on any one letter. After a moment, is slid down into the printed alphabet and paused.

"F...O...X" Helen read the letters aloud, her voice still playing to an audience of one.

"Yes, Adelaide, the fox. Who was the fox?" The planchette swirled again, zipping back and forth across the board. It came back to the letters.

"D...A...N...G...E...R" Helen read aloud again.

"Yes, Adelaide, I believe you. There is danger. But from who?"

"C...R...Y...S...T...A...L..." Helen's voice was getting louder though her pitch was staying flat

"Is it someone named Crystal? Is that who infiltrated my dream? Adelaide, please!" Hedy's own voice sounded desperate

The planchette began to zip around the board, zigging and zagging so quickly that Helen could hardly manage to hold on to it with her fingertips.

"S...H...E....I...S...C...O...M...I...N...G.....L...Y... S...S...A...." The planchette flew from Helen's hand and smashed against the wall, the corner of the heart shape breaking off into a large splinter. Something didn't want them asking anymore questions.

# CHAPTER TWELVE

"Thank you, Helen. You were a great help. At least I know what I am dealing with now." Hedy watched Helen carefully step down the porch stairs, taking pains not to trip over the power cord that Darro had strung along for his circular saw. She would have to ask him to move it before someone tripped.

"My pleasure, Hedy. Sorry for leaving salt all over your carpet. Keep an eye out for any rogue poltergeists." With a wave of her average looking arm, Helen was gone.

Hedy hardly had time to think about what she had learned about Lyssa, the day was all going so quickly. In between preparing for tomorrow's Christmas market and helping the sharp uptick in customers, she was fielding questions about the special project she had commissioned from Darro and watching Raluca as she watched Hedy warily from the corner in the shop.

"Can I get you anything, Miss Vaduva?" Hedy asked again, sure the answer would still be no.

"Nothing that is available in your shop, I am afraid. What I require isn't for sale." She spoke with a weariness in her voice that surprised Hedy. Mel had the counter covered so Hedy came over to the woman's table.

"Do you need me to fetch something? I can run to the market." Hedy didn't want to hover over her, so she sat down at the table.

"No, it isn't like that. Moroi can't go to the local grocer for what they need. Well, not really. Unless you count the grocer himself." Raluca chuckled and her eyes looked like black pinpoints.

"I don't understand. I thought Moroi didn't drink...blood." The conversation was taking a decidedly dark turn.

"Moroi do not require blood to survive, as strigoi do and as did my parents. There are those Moroi who do drink, for its euphoric effects. It is much like a drug's effect for a mortal. I do not care to be enthralled to any substance, so I do not drink. But Moroi do still need something that humans possess. We lack our own source of energy, *suflet*...err spirit, yes, energy of the spirit. We need humans to provide it to us. I am in need of this." Raluca looked at Hedy in a matter of fact way, expecting neither fear nor revulsion, but just understanding. It is what she received.

"How do you acquire the energy? Does it hurt the person?" A couple came into the shop wearing matching sweaters with large Christmas llamas on them, and both Raluca and Hedy waited until they were out of earshot.

"No, it doesn't harm the human. They will be tired, yes, but they can replenish with rest and human contact. The transfer is rather simple, really. I only need to grasp the human with my hands and the energy leeches through the skin. The older I get, the more often I find I need the energy. When I was young, even into my second century, I could go weeks without any such feeding. But now, I find myself in need within a few days. Such is the price of age." Raluca chuckled and shook her head at the couple in their sweaters. Americans were so ridiculous.

"I am your host and part of my job is to see that you have what you need." Hedy reached her arm out toward Raluca and gave a sharp nod. The old woman studied her face, unsure how to accept the gesture.

"This will not affect my inspection results. You understand that?" Raluca saw Hedy's expression harden.

"If you knew me, you would know that such a thought would be insulting."

Raluca paused a few more moments in contemplation before taking Hedy's forearm within her own gnarled hands. Hedy's skin was warm and smooth beneath her palms. Raluca closed her eyes and pressed against Hedy, lightly clasping her arm. She felt the energy immediately; this woman radiated spirit and Raluca marveled at how easily it flowed from her. She could feel it passing through her skin quickly, flowing into Raluca and filling her like a flash flood on parched earth. She instantly felt revived and rejuvenated. If she wasn't careful, she could draw too much from her host, it was so free-flowing.

After several moments, Raluca released Hedy's arm and opened her eyes. Hedy looked a bit peaked, her face pale and lacking its usual rosy color. She had her eyes closed and seemed to be collecting herself.

"Does it hurt in any way?" Raluca knew the answer but she wanted Hedy to acknowledge that she was fine.

"No, it doesn't hurt. I feel...diminished. Smaller, if that makes sense. As if a candle is nearing the end of the wax. It makes me feel a bit shaky and...hungry." Hedy opened her eyes slowly and she was astonished to see the change in Raluca; the old woman looked ten years' younger easily, with flush in her cheeks and a shine in her eyes.

"You should eat something, and ask that young woman to give you an embrace. It will help. Thank you, Miss Leckermaul. I am grateful." Raluca nodded toward Hedy and she smiled a bit as she said Hedy's name. She wondered if the woman knew her name meant "sweet-toothed person" in German. She felt a twinge of guilt about her upcoming recommendation to close the waystation.

"I think I will go make myself some tea and eat a cookie. If you will excuse me." Hedy rose slowly from the table and made her way to the counter. The sharp-eyed Mel noticed Hedy looked the worse for wear and she gave Raluca a wary look. The old woman smiled slightly in return.

Thanks to Hedy, Raluca would have enough energy to finish her work here before heading back to Brussels. She needed to interview the undine, for form sake, before finishing her report. She also would meet with the current traveler and perhaps she could help with this local matter on her way out. Yes, that should all be resolved before she left, likely on Sunday.

It would be good to get home. This place was damp and gray and Raluca did not care for the rotting scent of pine trees in this state, let alone just being in America in general. No sense of propriety or tradition here.

The young girl was giving Hedy an embrace, of her own volition, and she could see the energy flow between them. The pair practically radiated, though they had no idea. It was fortunate for both of them that Moroi were as scarce as they were, or they would be besieged with them. They would be very tempting morsels indeed and Raluca could see either of them being kept as an energy *sclav*, a captive donor. Her parents had kept three for Raluca in their home near Bucharest.

"All better," she said though neither heard her. Now that she had Hedy's energy, Raluca could feel Hedy's presence across the room and she willed her to turn and look at her; Hedy looked across the room at Raluca and saw the old woman smile. The connection would fade soon enough. The doorbell tinkled again, more people were coming into the shop.

"These Americans and their sweets. Hmpf," Raluca muttered under her breath.

❊ ❊ ❊

Just before she called her guests to dinner, Hedy took advantage of the quiet and lit the Christmas tree. It was dusk and the dark outside was tinged with the glow of the Christmas lights along the roof line, set with a timer to come on once the sun had dipped below the horizon. Hedy left the entry lights off for the moment so she could just enjoy the silver glow from the tree, pouring out from the branches and reflecting on the spiderwebs. The soft glow of the German pyramid candles kept the room from being too dark, and in the quiet of the hall, away from the lights in the shop, Hedy could just sit for a moment and savor the beauty of it all.

She was still tired from her exchange with Raluca and it felt good to sit. She was also exhausted from her nightmare and the fitful sleep that followed it. As peaceful as the entry was and as glad as she was to be there, in the moment, taking it all in, Hedy was tired to the bone and she worried that she wouldn't have the energy to push through. She hadn't even spared a thought about Lyssa until now.

"She is danger. Know that." Hedy heard Adelaide's voice soft against her ear and the little hairs on her neck prickled at the voice and the message.

"Lyssa is back? Adelaide, where is she?" Hedy was so tired. How could she fight off Lyssa again? And this time without Bren. Where was he?

"Hedy, danger in threes. Watch her." Adelaide's voice was drifting away from Hedy; she knew because the room was warming up around her.

"Adelaide, I can't do this alone. I need help." The words weren't even out of her mouth and she knew no one would be answering. The room was warm again, with the scent of fresh pine and cinnamon, and warm candle glow meeting the silver glinting of the tree. The door chimed and Hedy rose tiredly from her seat, wanting to turn on the lights so the customers wouldn't trip in any shadows.

"Welcome to The Gingerbread Hag. Please, come in." Hedy smiled and gestured for the couple to enter the shop. She could smell the scent of her Hungarian goulash coming from the kitchen. She would need to see to Raluca and Yami before she could finish the night and the thought of an evening of chit-chat with Yami and stern glances from Raluca sounded a bit too much for Hedy at the moment.

She would try her best, but tonight, her best might not be good enough.

# CHAPTER THIRTEEN

*The night before - Thursday*

Yami had to find Lyssa, which was no easy thing. Lyssa's method was to contact Yami, not the other way around, and Yami had no idea where Lyssa was holing up. She thought the first place she should look would be any abandoned houses, somewhere that Lyssa could stay and not risk exposure. Yami thought about the lot just next door, where the remnants of a fire were still visible, but the house itself was gone and the land was being prepped for new construction. Lyssa wouldn't be there.

Being a city girl, she tried her ride sharing app, hailing a ride to take her to the grocery store on the other side of town.

"Heading to Safeway, yes?" The woman was pleasant enough, even if her car did have the faint odor of stale tobacco. She must have been a smoker.

"Yes I am. But I am really interested in abandoned houses; I like to photograph them. Do you know of any around town?"

"Hmmm, there aren't too many. Property is valuable right now, with all the folks from Seattle looking to move out here. It's the view of the mountain and a lower house price that draws 'em." The woman made little humming noises as she thought. "Oh, well, you saw the empty lot next to where I picked you up. That was burned down a couple of months ago, but they are already prepping to build again, mortgage company didn't waste any time. There is one that's close to Safeway, though. I'll drive you by it and you can see it."

The woman took a turn which caused her GPS to reroute her; the ride share app had already calculated her fastest route. There was a row of little houses, likely built in the early twentieth century, but lacking much of the craftsman charm of many of their neighbors. These looked the worse for wear, with peeling paint and sagging roofs. The driver pulled up in front of the one on the end of the row, a large orange sign plastered on its front door.

"It was seized; they were making meth in there. Whoever owns the paper on that one will have to rehab it down to the studs before they can sell. It's been empty for the better part of a year. Did you want to take a picture?" The woman sounded rather bewildered with the question.

"No, this isn't quite what I am looking for."

Yami could tell right away that Lyssa wasn't here; her presence was easy for Yami to pick up on.

Having had her tour of the former meth house of Enumclaw, Yami was dropped off at the grocery store with no idea where to look next. It was getting dark and no doubt Hedy and the old woman were still chattering away.

"I can make use of the time while I find Lyssa," Yami thought and she started walking away from the town, toward the pastures and farms of nearby Buckley.

About a mile away from the store, there was a highway that led drivers toward Buckley, but Yami wasn't going that way. She veered off, finding her way into a small thicket of scrub brush and cattails. She squatted down to avoid being seen and removed all her clothes, leaving them in a neat pile, hidden from view.

Yami began her transformation, closing her eyes and drawing in the air around her. She could feel the bristles of fur piercing her skin and the strange sensation of her bones realigning into her true form. It didn't hurt but it wasn't pleasant; the change brought so many sensations all at once, it was overwhelming. She could suddenly smell everything, hear everything - how dull the human senses were in comparison. She was now encased in reddish fur and both of her long tails wrapped around her. As a kitsune, she would gain tails throughout her long years until she finally reached nine of them.

Yami shook her body and felt every hair move. She was fully in her true form and ready to continue on toward Buckley and the farms that were waiting.

Traveling much faster in fox form, Yami ran along the trails that crisscrossed the land between Enumclaw and Buckley. Full darkness had set in, but she could keenly see any obstacles before her. She reached the small goat farm, easily smelling their presence along the way. Standing up briefly on her hind legs, she used one paw to hold the latch up and another to pull it forward. The gate wasn't even locked. She crept in and the small herd of goats began rustling and making noise. She glanced over at the house and no lights flickered on. Apparently, these part-time farmers weren't home from their day jobs yet. No one would be coming to help the goats.

Yami was swift, dispatching each nanny goat with ease. Yami was larger than any natural fox, and she used her size to pin the animals down, looking calmly into their strange rectangular pupils. She saw panic and wild fear in them, so she did her best to make the end quick for them. Painless, it was not, but it was at least quick.

The herd was dispatched and Yami's fur was covered in their blood. She had seen a small wallow just down the road, full of rainwater, and she ran there to wash her fur clean, taking care especially around her muzzle. She gave her fur a violent shake; despite the cold air and being drenched, she wasn't cold. One task done, it was time to search again for Lyssa.

Yami ran back along the trails, heading toward Enumclaw. She had no idea if Lyssa was even nearby. She would search a bit more but if she couldn't find her, she would just have to pursue the course she thought best, which was killing the old woman. Surely, Lyssa would appreciate the chaos that would come from killing a leader of the waystations. And if Lyssa didn't like it, there really wouldn't be much she could do about it. She would have herself to blame for being inaccessible.

Yami returned to the spot where she had hidden her clothing and it was all still there, if a bit damp from sitting on the wet ground. With no small measure of reluctance, she began the transformation again back to human form. Shapeshifting took tremendous energy and she knew there would be a price to pay. She tried not to concentrate on the crackling of her bones or the sudden chill that surrounded her naked skin with the fur now gone. Becoming human was always more unpleasant for Yami.

She quickly drew her clothing back on, making sure she stayed below the sight line of the scrub bushes before finally standing up and giving a long stretch. Someone driving by did a double take as he saw her stand, but she just smiled. Wouldn't he have a funny story to tell.

"Well, now what?" Yami started walking back

along the road toward town. She should never have taken this job. Her skill set was geared toward assassination or quick in and out thefts, not just infiltrating and watching. Watching for what? What did Lyssa want her to do? The host, Hedy, was eccentric but she seemed harmless. The Moroica was another story.

The sky was almost dark now but Yami could make out the silhouette of a group of birds, swirling and flying low. They looked like crows. Perhaps not so unusual near a roadway where they could scavenge, but these crows were peculiar. Yami watched them sway and dive in unison, as if almost giving a collective wave, beckoning her to follow them. They were swooping and diving back toward the direction of that park where she met Lyssa.

"Of course, she uses crows. That is so clear," Yami muttered as she started to jog to follow the birds, glad she had worn flat shoes and not the heels she favored. No one driving by seemed to notice her or the strange flock of crows doing their dance in the sky.

It wasn't long before she saw the park, now completely in darkness. The street lights had come on but that area had none. The crows had dispersed into the blackness and Yami passed the last circle of light from the lamps and stepped into the dark of the park.

"I see you got the message," Lyssa's voice called out to her from the vague direction of the large tree. Yami's eyes could see the shapes in the darkness, and she stepped a bit closer, but not too close. Best to always be on guard.

"Yes, they were rather easy to spot. Perhaps a telephone would be easier." Yami heard Lyssa chuckle.

"Oh, now where would be the fun in that. How many gods do you think have a wireless plan? My crows make good messengers. Now, let's discuss where things are."

Yami sensed rather than saw that Lyssa was moving closer to her. She instinctively reached for the short tanto knife she kept near her waistband.

"No need for that. We're friends here. So, Miss Leckermaul has a visitor. My crows saw her arrive. Is she truly Moroi?"

"Yes, she claims to be. Her name is Raluca Vaduva. She is high up in the Concierge hierarchy. She came to inspect the waystation after the incident involving you." Again, Yami heard Lyssa chuckle.

"How touching that the waystations have such concern for the welfare of the guests. It would be quite the thing if Miss Leckenmaul's waystation got closed down. A little tit for tat." Lyssa chuckled again.

"You could do more than that. According to the woman, she is the only one in the waystation network that knows the location of every house. You know that the Moroi have photographic memories, yes? Apparently, they have put hers to good use. No one else knows the locations of every waystation except this old woman." Yami heard Lyssa take a sharp breath.

"Oh, yes. Imagine if we knew where every waystation was located. One by one, each one destroyed, leaving no refuge for the guests but to turn out into the world…a world that doesn't know they exist. Imagine how much chaos that would bring and how easy it would be to inflame anger. Oh, it is too much of a gift. Perhaps it is a trap of some kind. Did the old woman know you were there?"

"She likely knows of my presence, but I haven't met her yet. I don't think there is much chance that she or Hedy knew I was eavesdropping; they were deep in conversation and, as you know, I can be quiet and tread lightly."

"Then this is the sign I have been waiting for. We must take the old woman and extract the locations from her. If she will not willingly tell us… well, we will have to use your unique talents." Lyssa was moving back against the tree and Yami realized she had been clenching her hands the whole time. She released them and gave them a shake. The air in the park was decidedly sour.

"What do you want me to do? I don't know how long she is going to be in town, but I suspect a few days." Yami didn't relish kidnapping; it often was too unpredictable and messy. But at least it would mean she would finish the job and could leave this town.

"Watch for an opportunity; it will present itself, surely. Try to wait until the old woman is alone. Once you have her, bring her to the woods. Just follow the signs east toward the Olson Tree Farm. There is a cave near there; my crows will guide you in. We will chat with her there. Oh, and don't forget to continue your havoc with the livestock. You'd be surprised how angry the locals are becoming."

Lyssa laughed again and was gone, slipping into the darkness and leaving Yami with no chance to ask questions.

"Damn, never again. After this job, I am done," she whispered as she left the dark of the park and returned to the street lights. She was in for a long night of prowling chicken coops and rabbit hutches, working for a madwoman.

# CHAPTER FOURTEEN

*Friday*

"Do ye have all ye need from me, then?" Darro had been working out on Hedy's porch all day and now that night was coming, he was eager to get home.

Hedy and Mel stared at the giant wooden spinning pyramid that he had constructed without saying a word; they were speechless.

Hedy had asked if he could make a large version of her traditional Christmas pyramid that was powered by the heat from candles spinning the large rotor at the top. She wanted something for the Christmas market that would showcase her treats and be eye catching. She thought he might be able to pull off a version perhaps twice as big as the normal table top one she had in her entry. Instead, he had created a behemoth that stood as tall as he was.

"Well, are you gonna stand mouths agape or you gonna say something? Will it do? I used a small motor to turn the blades since the kind of firepower you'd need in candles might burn down the whole place. I could have made it finer if I had more time but you said you wanted something rustic, and so it is. I used boughs and pine cones from the yard, and a bit of swirly trim from the hardware store. Do you like it?" For all the work he had done, he hoped she did because he wasn't prepared to make any changes.

"It is amazing, Darro. Absolutely amazing. Better and bigger than I could have hoped. Mel, look at those gnomes he has placed along the platforms. Honestly, it is perfect!" Hedy was as giddy as she had been in ages to see such a thing of beauty.

"How are we going to get it to the hall? It won't fit in the Corvair, that's for sure." Mel was still marveling at the slowly moving rotors at the top that were spinning the three platforms slowly.

"I can take it there for ye and assemble it. I'm in for a penny, in for a pound. Besides, I was going to go see the sights meself anyway. It will fit neatly in my truck." Darro hadn't worked with wood in years but he was glad to see he hadn't lost his touch. He had done well, if he did say so himself.

"Well, I can't thank you enough. It will be the hit of the market." Hedy came forward, and without a word, gave Darro a big hug, which he was not at all expecting. He bristled slightly but accepted it as gracefully as he was able.

"Oh, aye, payment will be thanks enough. I

gathered supplies yesterday and spent all day building today, so my usual rate for two days would be adequate." His rent was due and the extra would be welcome in the lean months of winter when gardening wasn't at its peak.

"Oh, I can do a bit better than that since you have gone above and beyond on this. Let me get my purse." Hedy went back inside just as the Christmas lights on the house flicked on. He had done a marvelous job installing those as well. What she would have done without Darro, she just didn't know.

"It truly is great, you know. And it made Hedy smile, which is a really good thing. She has seemed so down lately." Mel stepped down from the porch to admire the lights fully. The old house looked magnificent in the pinkish white bulbs and Darro had even encased the small shop sign at the curb in tiny twinkling pink lights. She would have to take a picture of it to show her mom. Ana would be seeing it in person.

"Aye, I noticed that meself. I thought perhaps she missed Skinny Malinky Longlegs himself, Bren. But I don't know if that is the cause. Perhaps she is just lonesome for company." Darro shuffled down the stairs and joined Mel in admiring his handiwork.

"I'm keeping an eye on her. Well, her and now my cousin. Did you hear about what happened at the tree farm last night?" Mel noticed several crows had just landed in the tree closest to the house, which seemed strange as there was no garbage or stray food lying about.

"Oh, aye, I heard about it when I was at the hardware store this morning. I also heard that the wee houligans have been causing havoc around town today. One of them was caught breaking windows at the library before school, another had tossed eggs at the principal's house - he was at the hardware store buying supplies to clean it all up. What's gotten into them?" Darro headed back up the stairs to wait for Hedy inside; it was getting a little chilly even for the Scotsman.

"I don't know. It must have been the scare of being in that cave. I am going to check on my cousin, Dylan, tonight to make sure he is okay and keeping out of trouble." Mel followed the big man onto the porch and into the entry, back into the cinnamon scented warmth of the house.

"St. Nick won't bring him any gifts if he acts up. He best remember that."

"I'll remind him when I call. Maybe the threat of no presents will get him back to his old self." Mel left Darro in the entry to get his money from Hedy. She walked quickly passed the strange old woman who had been watching her all day and back to the batch of peppermint brownies she was making. At least Anahita would be here tomorrow, and Mel was beyond excited to see her. She tried to put the worry for Dylan in the back of her mind, at least for the night.

* * *

Darro left with a loud “Ta” and Hedy turned to find Yami coming down the stairs. She hadn’t seen her all day and now it was night; the woman certainly kept strange hours.

“Yami, it's good to see you. You must be famished. Can I fix you something to eat?” Hedy waited for her guest to reach her in the entry.

“Yes, that would be nice. My apologies for not coming down sooner, I was sleeping in. I am more of a night owl.” Yami smiled at Hedy but she was also keenly aware of the old woman’s presence just inside the shop.

“I think the Hungarian goulash I made is about ready. We can sit down for a proper dinner. Oh, and let me introduce you to Miss Valuca.” Hedy led Yami into the shop and close to Raluca’s table. The Moroica had been reading a small book she had drawn out of her Coach handbag.

“Yami Hayashi, may I present Raluca Vaduva. She is visiting us for a few days.”

Yami extended her hand to shake, saying, “It is a pleasure to meet you, ma’am.” Raluca did not move.

“Please forgive me if I don’t take your hand; I never shake hands. I find the custom disgusting. Miss Hayashi, yes, I believe you have been a guest at our waystations before. It was in Dubai and also Warsaw, no?” Raluca gestured for Yami to sit down and she did so, with slight hesitation. It would be a challenge to deceive this woman about anything.

"I'll let you two get acquainted while I get dinner ready in the dining room." Hedy took her opportunity to exit gratefully. She hated to leave Yami alone in conversation with Raluca, but it was more awkward to hover nearby.

"Yes, I have been at both locations, though that was a few years ago. You have a remarkable memory to know the guests who stay at your waystations."

"It's true my memory is good, but in this case, I actually looked up your file as I knew I would be coming here. I am good, but not quite that good. Tell me, what do you think of this waystation? I am here to inspect and to judge; I could use your opinion." Raluca's hand was resting lightly on top of the small book and Yami could see the gnarled veins just below the surface.

"Hedy is a charming host. She has been very gracious and opened up her home to me. I have found her to be quite accommodating and attentive." Yami was being truthful with the old woman. Whether Lyssa wanted to destroy the network or not, Hedy had been nothing but kind to Yami.

"Well, that is good to hear. I have concerns that this...shop," Raluca waved her hand dismissively, "might be taking her away from her primary concern of caring for guests. I will take your thoughts under advisement." Raluca seemed to have dismissed Yami and the awkward pause seemed to confirm it.

Yami rose to leave, planning to assist Hedy in the dining room when Raluca spoke again.

“Oh...not that I particularly care, but your nocturnal activities are drawing concern in the community. I would suggest you cease, else you find yourself facing the barrel of a gun.” Raluca expression was rather blank for such a statement.

“I’m not sure what you mean, ma’am.” Yami had told no one at the Concierge that she was a kitsune. There would be no way for this Moroica to know.

“Oh, let’s not pretend, shall we? I know very well you are a kitsune. And no, I didn’t read it in a file. You think a Moroi wouldn’t know from the scent of your blood? There isn’t a creature in this world I can’t identify from scent. Their blood is their signature. And you, Miss Hayashi, are a kitsune of some advanced years; the scent of fox is strong but still your human blood is there as well. Do me the courtesy of honesty.” Raluca raised a penciled eyebrow at the woman who looked so surprised standing before her.

“As you say, I am a kitsune. But I know nothing of attacks-”

Raluca held up her hand to stop her. “Please, don’t lie. The smell of the animal blood permeates you. Again, you dishonor me with your lying. I will forgive it as you are used to having to hide your nature from all those around you. I give you a friendly warning; you would do well to stop these attacks before you find yourself in a trap or worse. That is the last I will say on it."

Raluca had dismissed her, opening the cover of her book again. She found the tawdry nature of lying too exhausting; what was the point of it all. The kitsune left her without another word and she hoped the woman heeded her warning. She would not wish a guest of the waystations to find herself caught in some common trap. Worse still, if Miss Hayashi was killed in her fox form, she would change back to human and then what a mess that would be.

"'Let no one be slow to seek wisdom when he is young,' as Epicurus would say. Let's hope she heeds the wisdom," Raluca muttered as she returned to her book of ancient philosophers.

# CHAPTER FIFTEEN

The cave was dark, which is how she liked it. Dark except for the slight orange glow of the crystal deep in the tunnel. She relished the dark. It was the perfect place for her to recuperate and draw power. The crystal seemed to make her stronger, both her form and her ability to manipulate humans. She'd learned that when the children wandered into the cave. How easy it had been to whisper in their ears, to set them on the path that leads to anger and destruction. She laughed at the thought of it. Her very own "Yule lads" wreaking havoc on those around them with every spiteful kick or toppled tree.

Yes, the Moroica would serve her purposes well and even escalate her goals, with all that delectable knowledge just tucked away in that ancient brain of hers. Lyssa could only imagine how hard the Moroica would fight to keep her secrets and it made her smile; her kitsune would have to extract each detail, one by one, and Lyssa would enjoy the process. Once she had wrung all the information out of her, they would snuff her out like an ancient candle and Lyssa would be nearly ready to return to the world.

The crystal was helping her heal, she was sure of that. It was only a matter of time before she would be well enough to proceed with her dark purpose.

* * *

Dylan slipped out of the house after dinner. He was supposed to be upstairs, playing Nintendo, but he crawled out his window and climbed down from the porch roof. He was supposed to meet up with the group and he didn't want to miss this.

"You're late." Harley sounded annoyed. They met in the alley behind a row of shops in town.

"I'm here now, so quit bitching. You ready?" Dylan would never have talked back to Harley, or really anyone, before. But now, he just didn't care. What could they do to him?

"You are lucky I like you, Dylan, or I'd give you a beat down. I still might." Harley chuckled, which caused Randy to laugh as well. Tamara didn't join in.

"Are we doing this or what?" She was impatient to get started.

"Yeah, let's get the party started. Everybody bring gloves?" Harley watched them all waive their pairs in the air. "Good. I brought rocks in this backpack. I also brought this." He waved a baseball bat toward them. "Apparently, this is a Christmas present for me from my dad."

Harley laughed again and this time all of them joined in.

"Ok, time for a little smash and grab. Put your hoods on and get a mask from Randy." Harley signaled for Randy, who pulled out a plastic bag that had Halloween masks. Harley reached in and grabbed one that looked like the Joker.

"Let's go smash things up."

Dylan grabbed the last mask, disappointed that he was left with Iron Man. He tied his sweatshirt hood tight around his face and grabbed some rocks from Harley's bag. He couldn't wait to hear the glass shatter.

The kids rounded the corner from the small alley where they had put on their masks, following Harley's lead. The shop closest to them had soaps and lotions, and Dylan thought the name was hilarious; who named a store the Owl and the Jam Jar? Harley took his bat and smashed the window, glass shards flying into the air and scattering on the sidewalk at their feet. Dylan was glad he was looking through the plastic slits of the Iron Man's mask since it kept the glass away from his face.

The window display had nothing that any of them wanted but that wasn't really the point. It was the destruction, the wonderful sound of smashing and breaking with nothing and no one to stop them. Harley pulled bottles from the wooden shelves and was stomping them into oblivion, the scent of fruit and honey splattered against the ground and the walls, even into the tiny nose holes of Dylan's mask. It wouldn't be long before their presence was known; they would have to keep moving if they were going to smash up the whole street.

"What's next?" Dylan heard Randy's muffled voice from his mask, which was Spiderman. Harley was having all the fun and the others wanted in on the action.

"Next door, smash it up." Tamara's voice came out from the Ninja Turtle mask she had on and it sounded so harsh that Dylan almost didn't recognize it. He liked the sound of her, all gruff and mean.

Dylan had a crowbar inside his jacket, and he thought it was time to smash some glass for himself. He brushed past Harley, who was still stomping bottles of lotion, and raised the bar to throw it into the window. He had plans for lighting the mannequin in the fuzzy sweater on fire and he could almost imagine how good the burning plastic would smell. His arm was high above his head, ready to strike, when someone grabbed it.

It was Harley.

"No. Not that one. Leave that one alone." Harley's jeans were soaked in lotion up to his knees.

"What for?" Dylan could taste his disappointment; it was fogging the inside of his mask.

"Not that one, okay? I just got a feeling. We shouldn't do that one. Leave it alone and move on." Harley's voice left no room for argument. Dylan felt sure if he disobeyed, Harley would be stomping him into the pavement instead of lotion bottles.

"Weirdo. Whatever. I'm moving on." Dylan shrugged like he didn't care but secretly, inside his mask, he was grimacing at Harley and making terrible faces of rage. How dare he tell Dylan what to smash? It wouldn't be long before Dylan would get even with him and then he'd be back to finish things off at that stupid store with the Red Bat on the front door. What made that store so special?

When Harley's back was turned, Dylan stepped forward and put his hand on the door handle. A wave of revulsion coursed through him; he could taste the bile rising in his mouth. He couldn't have moved his hand any faster if it had been on fire.

"Dylan, you coming?" he heard Tamara's muffled voice calling to him.

"Yeah, I'm coming." He shuddered slightly and followed the trio down the street.

# CHAPTER SIXTEEN

Saturday arrived after an awkward evening and Hedy was grateful it was behind her. Yami had barely appeared before she found an excuse to head back to her room. Raluca had gone to her room as well after passing on the Hungarian goulash as too spicy and inauthentic. It was just as well as far as Hedy was concerned; she was still tired from her donation to Raluca and she needed sleep. She had closed up shop early and fallen into a deep but troubled sleep. She was glad at least there had been no more nightmares. She'd had her fill of foxes.

Today would be a busy one. They had to pack up all the baking as well as the giant pyramid and get over to the expo hall by three o'clock to set up. Darro promised he would be over an hour early to help with the loading and Mel was going to meet them at the hall after picking up Anahita at the train station in Auburn and bringing her into town for the day.

Hedy was also quite excited, if she were being

honest with herself, to see Michael again. She hoped she would have an opportunity to wander by his stall, wearing her new outfit.

"Hedy, have you noticed…I mean, I don't know why you would, it probably isn't important. But have you noticed the crows outside?" Alice was perched by the open window in the kitchen where she had just come in from.

"Crows? No, Alice, I haven't noticed. Do you mean right now?" Hedy gave a peek out into the dark morning light, but she saw nothing.

"Yes. I mean no. I mean yes and no. They started arriving last night and there are more today."

"Hmmm, no I can't say I have noticed. I wonder if there is a dead animal in the yard that is attracting them." Hedy thought of Ren and hoped it wasn't him.

"No, I don't think so. I would likely smell it and I don't smell it, so I don't think so. They are just sitting near the house, watching." Alice gave a little shudder.

"Well, can you ask them what they want?" Hedy didn't know if that was even possible, but she assumed birds in different species had way to communicating.

"I…could…try but you know crows. Or maybe you don't know crows but I know crows and they are so…snooty. Really unlikeable birds, if you ask me. But I suppose there is no harm in trying." Alice gulped slightly. The harm might be that they would try to eat her, or at least that was her worry.

"Well, don't put yourself to any bother over it, Alice. Maybe they are just resting up to fly somewhere else. If they start causing trouble, we can deal with it then. Have some breakfast and take your mind off it." Hedy put out a small plate of granola for Alice and she hopped down to the table.

"Yes, I suppose it could be nothing, just me being silly. Silly Alice," she chirped and tucked into the granola. There was likely nothing going on, Alice told herself. It wasn't as if she was a smart bird, she knew that, so why would she be noticing anything that was really peculiar or dangerous. Surely, Hedy or even Zelda would know far faster than she would. *Silly Alice*, she thought.

"Just the same, I'll take a little walk outside to see what I see. Thank you for keeping an eye on the house. It is always good to have someone on watch." She gave Alice a light stroke on her back feathers and Alice chirped again.

"Of course, Hedy, any time. But you should ask that clever Zelda to take a look. Zelda would know straight away."

"Yes, maybe I'll do that. Thank you, Alice." Hedy poured her cup of coffee and headed toward the front of the house. It was just light enough outside that she should be able to see what Alice was on about.

It was cold and damp out; the kind of cold that quickly gets inside your bones. Hedy pulled her cardigan around her a little tighter and carefully stepped down the stairs toward the garden. She would have to ask Darro to add some rubber treads to the stairs, so they weren't so slick in the rain.

Sure enough, the large tree in the yard did have an extraordinarily large number of crows. They were perched silently in the tree, still and watching. Even when she came closer, they didn't flutter or caw or even move as if they saw her.

"Very peculiar. Alice was right." Hedy gave a few large sniffs to see if she could smell carrion but there was nothing but the damp spongy smell of wet grass, wood chips, and earth. Well, at least that means it isn't Ren out here, she thought. She headed back inside, away from the cold and the weird silent birds watching her.

She found Raluca inside, sitting at her usual table in the bakery. Today's suit was a pale pearl, which made Raluca's black hair look all the darker. Her skin still looked flushed, which must mean that Hedy's energy was still there supporting her.

"Good morning, Miss Vaduva. I hope you slept well. Would you care for some coffee or tea?" Hedy forced herself to look cheerful. She wasn't really mentally ready for more questions or chit chat with the Moroica.

"Your coffee is too strong for me. I would take a cup of tea, though. Thank you. Once I have met with Miss Sohrab, I will complete my report and be on my way. She is arriving today, yes?" Raluca accepted the cup of tea with a slight nod of her head.

"Yes, she will be coming for the Christmas market. Mel will be picking her up at the train station and bringing her to town. After the market, she is going to come back here."

"That should suffice. I had hoped she might arrive earlier so that I could depart today, but it seems I shall be your guest one more night." Raluca pursed her lips after tasting the tea; it was not as fresh as it could be.

"You might wish to join us at the market today; it should be quite entertaining." Hedy spoke with her back slightly turned toward Raluca, busying herself with gathering up the travel containers. She could well imagine the old woman's sour look.

"I will content myself with my reading. I find the ancient philosophers to be quite relevant. As I come closer to my own end, though I have had many centuries to prepare for it, I find myself seeking wisdom in the words of those long gone. 'Death does not concern us, because as long as we exist, death is not here. And when it does come, we no longer exist.' Epicurus' words are as true today as they were two thousand years ago." Raluca's voice had taken on a bit of a softer tone, causing Hedy to turn to look at her.

"Surely you have years ahead of you, Miss Vaduva. I would imagine you will be visiting waystations and writing reports well into the future." And terrifying hosts, thought Hedy.

"No, this is my last such adventure. I have

known my energy was dwindling for some time, but this journey has proved that I am not physically able to work in the field. It is of no matter. I can work at the Concierge, training the one who will replace me. Another Moroi, naturally." Raluca gave a delicate sniff.

"Does the one you are training have to visit each waystation personally?" Hedy could only imagine how long that would take.

"No, to learn the locations of every waystation does not require travel to them, though it is encouraged. My protégé will be doing much traveling in the days ahead but he will continue to learn the map from me."

Hedy was feeling bold since Raluca seemed to be in a chatting mood, so she decided to take a chance with a question. "If you don't mind me asking, I have wondered something. Since the Concierge contacts the host that a traveler is coming, wouldn't the caller have the phone numbers of all the waystations right there? You said that only you know the location of all the waystations." Hedy watched Raluca smile.

"Clever girl to ask. But no, our callers do not actually dial the number. Each waystation is assigned a code name and the caller enters the code name into the system, which dials the number. I am the only one with access who can add or delete waystations from the system. No one else has the full knowledge of just how many there are or where they are located. A traveler tells us where they want to go and one of my assistants provides the itinerary and code names to the callers, who contact the hosts. My assistants and my protégé know enough to manage in my absence but his training is not complete."

Hedy thought she might be pressing her luck to ask anything further. Her suspicion was confirmed by Raluca opening the cover to her book. She had to ask one more thing, though.

"What's the code name for this waystation?" Hedy saw Raluca smile slightly but she did not look up.

"Cookie. It's cookie."

# CHAPTER SEVENTEEN

"I'm here, ready to load." Darro's voice broke the silence that had settled over the shop. Hedy was busy preparing, and Raluca was reading. Yami, true to form, was nowhere to be seen.

"Great, I'm almost packed up. Do you want me to help you load the Pyramid?"

"Ah, I can manage. I built it, dinna I? It comes in sections, so it won't be a bother to load. I'll have it now. Are you feeding those crows or something? The old foosty tree in the front is chock-a-block with them." Darro peered out the window, though the tree wasn't visible from there.

"No, I don't know what is going on with those crows. I noticed them this morning after a little bird told me." Hedy smiled. "I thought you might have an idea what is going on."

"Nothing that I've done in the garden should have raised this ruckus. Perhaps someone cut down their normal roosting tree. You need your cat out there to roust them about."

"Well, I suspect she wouldn't be very willing to take on that job, but I can ask her. Anyway, I'll finish up packing up these totes and start bringing them to the porch, okay?" Darro nodded as he went back out the door. It took him a moment to remember that in this house, Hedy *could* actually ask the cat.

Hedy could hear Darro's singing over the sound of the pyramid pieces clanking down on the porch. She didn't understand what he was saying, but the tune sounded like a Scottish lullaby.

"Mo ghaol, mo ghradh,
a's m' fheudail thu,
M' ion'ntas ur a's n' eibhneas thu,
Mo mhacan aluinn ceutach thu,
Cha 'n fhiu mi fein bhi 'd dhail"

"I wonder what that means." Hedy hardly realized she had spoken the thought out loud.

"It's a Christmas song. Christ's Lullaby, I believe it is called," Raluca spoke up for the first time in hours.

"Oh, you speak Gaelic?"

Raluca laughed. "Certainly not. I did spend some time in Edinburgh one winter. It is a long story involving a traveler, a Wulver, who was causing commotion during his visit. My memory is such that when I hear a song, I remember it. Even when sung poorly."

Hedy laughed and surprisingly, Raluca joined her. It was the first time Hedy had heard her actually laugh. It wasn't a pleasant sound.

"Well, Darro doesn't have much of a singing voice but he is a terribly nice man and we like him quite a bit around here."

"Indeed. He seems like an…earthy fellow, this Darro. And poor singing or not, it is nice to be reminded of that December in Scotland."

Hedy started carrying the large rubber totes to the porch for Darro to load. She was bringing all the treats that she and Mel had been making in surplus over the last few days, as well as a whole container of lacy paper doilies to place on the rough shelves of the pyramid. She had thought about bringing coffee in thermos containers but decided against it. There would be enough to keep track of at the booth without worrying about hot coffee.

Walking into the entry, she looked at the Christmas decorations and decided she needed to bring a few with her, to finish off the booth, but most of her decorations were too fragile or valuable to risk damage. She gently touched the large bowl of nineteenth century mercury glass ornaments from Bohemia; there is no way they would stand up to the handling.

"What should I bring for the table, huh, Zelda?" The cat was passing through on her way to the kitchen.

"Nothing you would care about getting broken or stolen," Zelda said curtly as she continued on.

"Some help she is."

But Hedy knew she was right. While she wouldn't want any of her collection to be destroyed, some things were more valuable than others. On the small table near the tree, she noticed the grouping of ceramic elves. They were in shades of pearlescent pinks and greys, with a shimmering silver snowflake on each of their heads, like some strange hat. There were four of them; she had picked them up in a flea market and they probably dated from the 1950s. She liked them because they had a vaguely sinister look about their faces, with their black eyes and slightly sneering smiles.

"Yes, I think you lot will go nicely with the Krampus cookies. You do look a bit mischievous." Hedy gathered them up to find a small box she could tuck them into.

"Anything else to go to the hall?" Darro came huffing in, red cheeked like Santa himself.

"Just me. Parking is going to be tight so I thought maybe I could ride over with you?" Darro gave her a nod; there was room in the cab for her.

"Great. Give me a few minutes to change and I'll be ready. Help yourself to some coffee while you wait."

"I'll wait in the hall, if it's all the same to ye." He lowered his voice dramatically. "That one in there gives me the heebie-jeebies."

"She is fine, when you get to know her a bit." Hedy knew she was stretching it a bit to put Darro at ease, but he wasn't having it.

"All the same. I'll wait here."

Hedy hurried upstairs to change into her new

outfit from Michael's shop.

She took the red dotted swiss dress from the wardrobe and felt the same shiver of pleasure as the first time she saw it. It was adorable and she loved it. What was even better was that someone could pick that out for her, someone who didn't know her, and have it be really what she wanted. Hedy felt seen and understood, which for Hedy was rare.

She slipped the dress on over her head, careful to keep her bouffant hairstyle from getting smashed. She buttoned the high ruffled collar and gave herself a twirl in front of the mirror. "Just needs a few little touches." She had two small jeweled poinsettia clips that she added to her hair and then she slipped into her knee-high white patent leather go-go boots. Pleased with the final result, she headed back down to meet up with Darro and head to the hall to set up.

"You look like a Christmas elf from 1965," Zelda dryly remarked as Hedy passed her chair near the landing.

"That's right, and that is exactly what I wanted." Hedy didn't know if Zelda meant it as a complement or not, and she didn't care. She felt marvelous.

"Aren't you a sight all decked in red and white? Quite fetching, that." Darro gave her a smile as Hedy grabbed her cape from the coat rack.

"Thank you, Darro. I like to be festive. Shall we go?" Hedy stepped quickly into the shop to see

Raluca. "I'll be at the market for a while but there is barley and mushroom soup in the crockpot behind the counter, if you care for a bowl. Help yourself to anything you'd like. I'll be back this evening with Anahita."

"I shall see you then," was Raluca's reply, without a glance out of her book.

Hedy switched the sign to closed and locked the front door behind her without noticing Yami coming down the stairs.

Darro's truck had the stale aroma of pot, which always reminded Hedy of a skunk. It also was badly in need of shocks, so they jostled and bumped their way along the road until they reached the fairgrounds and expo hall on the eastern edge of town, with Darro breaking it up with more Scottish Christmas songs.

"Here ye are. Looks like quite the gathering already." Darro pulled into the dirt parking area, which already had quite a few vehicles.

"Must be the vendors getting set up. The event opens to the public in ninety minutes or so." Hedy carefully stepped from the truck, trying to keep her boots from getting dirty in the damp soil. There were patches of grass that served like stepping stones for her.

"I brought a dolly, so I can load up the totes and get you started while I bring in the pyramid. I'll meet ye at the entrance."

Hedy maneuvered her way through the cars and the wet dirt, finding her path to the front. A frazzled woman was there, checking names off a list and pointing as she spoke. Hedy reached her as the last vendor left her table.

"Yes?" The woman didn't look up from her list.

"Checking in. Hedy Leckermaul, The Gingerbread Hag." Hedy had a flash of annoyance. Would it really take that much energy to say hello?

"Ummmm, oh yes, here you are. Booth 53. You are on the west side of the hall." She took her red pen and made a giant circle on a paper map. "The table is numbered. Make sure you are set up before the event starts and no take down until 7:00 PM."

Finally, the woman looked up to hand Hedy the map, and her eyes opened a bit wider.

"Aren't you festive? That's what we like to see, costumes."

Hedy took the map she offered, without comment.

She paused at the entrance for Darro, who was pulling the dolly through the dirt. The hall was a huge barn like structure, with no doors on either end, and large overhead lights illuminating the space. During the summer fair, it housed the vegetable competitions, prize winning pies and 4 H displays.

"All set?" Darro had reached her, drawing his own share of looks as he pulled the dolly through the line.

"Yes, Miss Congeniality over there gave me the booth number. We are 53, on the west side." Hedy led the way into the hall, scanning the tables for her number. Many of the booths were already set up or well on their way; she worried that they had cut things too short.

"Looks like they have you grouped with the sausage vendor and that farm that sells the goat cheese and lotions. There's 53, right on the corner. That's a good spot." Darro spotted it first and he was right. The pyramid would be visible from two sides, which would really make it stand out.

"I'll start bringing in the wood pieces if you can handle the totes, yes?" Hedy nodded and Darro trudged off toward the entrance. He would have to make the trip three times to get all the pieces in.

Hedy started to unpack, and she was glad the first tote had the tablecloth. Most of the treats were going to be stacked up on the pyramid but she did bring several three-tiered stands so she could have samples of everything close by for viewing. With the table covered, she set up the stands and placed the eerie snowflake elves near them. She also set up the wooden tray stacked with napkins. The lockbox for making change was hidden within a tote under the table but she expected most customers to use their credit cards; no one seemed to have cash anymore.

"The Gingerbread Hag." A woman, stepping back to view her own display nearby, read the vinyl banner slowly aloud with what seemed to be disbelief. "That's a strange name indeed." She finished by flashing a tight smile at Hedy.

"Yes, indeed. Strange, much like my treats. I

cater to customers who like interesting things, not run of the mill." Hedy flashed her own smile, hoping she matched the woman's tone. Hedy had no interest in people who were rude.

"Well, let's hope you have good luck with the sales today. Hard to say with a crowd like this. You know, down to earth people." She gave Hedy a scanning look and moved away from the table. Hedy couldn't understand people who thought they were that superior to others.

"Hmmm, well, we will see, won't we?" Hedy took a deep breath and turned her attention back to unpacking.

Darro finished hauling in the last of the pyramid pieces and, faster than she expected, Hedy was looking at the finished product. It looked just as impressive as before, especially when he turned on the small motor that made the propeller turn slowly.

"There she is. Everything looks good and ready for your wares." He turned off the motor so the pyramid would be still for Hedy to load it up.

"It really is great, Darro. I'll get it loaded up with the treats and then we'll be ready to turn it back on. Thank you for everything. You have been such a big help." She gave him a quick squeeze on the arm.

"My pleasure, lass. Now, unless you need me, I am going to take a quick stroll through the place and then head home for a bit. I'll be back before the end though to help with taking her down."

"See you later." Hedy watched him head back toward the main door, taking the dolly with him. He grabbed a sample of sausage from the nearby table as he went.

She wouldn't have much time to get everything arranged but Mel should be there any minute with Anahita. Hedy pulled out the paper doilies and covered the three shelves of the pyramid, so that none of the underlying wood was visible. With her tongs in hand, she unpacked plastic boxes of treats and arranged each row of the pyramid. In short order she had stacks of Krampus cookies, peppermint bark brownies, bags of reindeer kibble and rum balls, and the highlight, her *Pfeffernüsse* cookies. Pleased with the lay out, she flipped the motor switch and the whole thing began to turn very slowly.

"Well, that's quite the display, I must say. You will put the rest of us to shame." She recognized Michael's voice and turned to see him standing near the table, holding one of the snowflake elves.

"Yes, I had a great deal of help from my friend, Darro. He built the pyramid. You look dapper in your Christmas vest, Michael. And I see you found my elves." Hedy smiled and watched him place the figurine back carefully near the stand.

"Yes, it gave me the idea of a snowflake fascinator hat. And you look marvelous in your new dress. It was just the right choice. It suits you perfectly." Hedy's cheeks flushed slightly.

"Well, my compliments to you for selecting it.

I was told I look like a Christmas elf from 1965 and I think that is rather accurate." She chuckled.

"Santa should be so lucky to have such a pretty elf. Sorry to leave so soon but it looks like they are starting to let people into the hall, so I better get back to my booth. I'm across the way, on the other side, booth 12. Look for the mannequin wearing the green velvet cocktail dress; you can't miss me." Michael gave her a wave and snatched a cookie from the tray in front. "You said I could have a cookie, remember?" he called back to her over his shoulder.

# CHAPTER EIGHTEEN

With Hedy gone, the house was quiet. Yami came down the stairs and opened the wooden gate that kept general customers away from the upstairs. Despite the squeaky floors, she had a light tread and she would be surprised if the old woman would hear her approach. She had zip ties and a small scarf in her hand to bind and gag her.

In the quiet, she noticed the rhythmic ticking of the grandfather clock. It sounded strangely loud when so often it was drowned out by the constant noise of the shop. Yami actually found it rather soothing, like an undercurrent or pulse for the house. Perhaps she should get such a clock for her apartment in Tokyo.

She came around the corner to see Raluca engrossed in her book, a cup of tea sitting near her on the table. The old woman looked small and hardly a risk for Yami. She had handled far bigger and more dangerous targets in the past.

"There you are. I was wondering when you

would come down. Have you ceased your nocturnal activities, Kitsune?" The old woman looked up from her book to give a skeptical eye to Yami. Did she know what was about to happen?

"I have a job to do here, although it is almost done, I am glad to say. My employer hired me to cause havoc in this town and now she insists on meeting you. I hope you will come willingly. I would hate to make this unpleasant." Yami spoke evenly, keeping her voice low and without threat. She wasn't very familiar with Moroi and what they might be able to do, even an old one such as this.

"Your employer? I see. So, you are here beyond just traveling, there is some ulterior purpose. Well, I suppose that makes more sense than a kitsune risking exposure to attack some random animals. And just who is your employer?" Raluca closed her book and folded her hands on top of the cover.

"Her name is Lyssa. She is the one who brought you here, since you are investigating the events from a few months ago. She is quite interested in meeting you and has commanded me to bring you to her. As I said, I don't want this to be unpleasant. Will you come willingly?"

This time, Yami brought the zip ties out from behind her back.

"Naturally. There is no reason for violence. I will meet her. Why doesn't she just come here? It would be easier than dragging an old woman to some meeting." Raluca's eyes were black pins staring through slits.

"Lyssa, as you know, was wounded in her last encounter. It has made her...more dangerous, frankly. I suggest we get in the car and make our way to her now. There is no reason this needs to be unpleasant for anyone." Yami placed the zip ties in her pocket, keeping her other hand on the small knife she had concealed in the other.

"Oh, no, let's keep things civil, by all means. Lead the way, Miss Hayashi. Let's get this over with, as I have things to do before I leave." Raluca stood up slowly and walked toward the front door, keeping a wide berth from Yami.

In her youth, it would have been nothing to dispatch this kitsune with a simple grip on her arm, sucking the very life energy from her. But now, Raluca wasn't so sure she would win the encounter. Easier to see what this Lyssa wanted.

"We will borrow Hedy's car. I'm sure she won't mind. It isn't far from here. Do I have your word I won't need to tie you up or restrain you in any way? I would really dislike it if you tried something while we were driving." Yami's last words edged with steel.

"You have my word that I will go willingly to meet this creature. Let's get this over with." The old woman found her pashmina on the coat rack and wrapped it tightly around her. The kitsune opened the door for her, which she found oddly polite for a kidnapper.

# CHAPTER NINETEEN

Even in a large hall like this, it started to get noisy quickly, with the sound of kids and adults coming in through the front entrance. The large open space and metal walls reverberated the sound and in no time, it was difficult for Hedy not to pick up snatches of conversations as people came by.

"Did you see all the windows boarded up on Wells Street? Someone smashed them out last night."

"Hit almost every store for two blocks. Glass was everywhere."

"Did they catch anyone?"

"I heard one of the shops had a surveillance camera, but they were wearing masks. Looked like kids."

The voices floated by, but Hedy was struck by the thought of all that damage. Michael's shop was on Wells, but he didn't mention anything happening to The Red Bat. She would have to ask him about it when she went to see his booth.

"Looks like you could use a hand." Hedy heard Mel's voice and turned to see both her and Anahita coming toward the booth. It had only been a few months since Hedy had seen the girl, but she went out and gave Ana a huge hug.

"It is so good to see you. We've missed you around here. How is Seattle?"

Anahita returned the hug and gave Hedy a quick peck on the cheek. "Good to see you, too. Seattle is fine. I found an apartment near the University and I'm settling in. It's nice to be back in town, though."

Ana gave Mel a meaningful look and Hedy couldn't help but smile at the two girls.

"Well, things look like they are starting to pick up, so if you don't mind helping out for a bit, I wouldn't say no to the help." Both girls nodded and followed Hedy behind the table, pausing to look at the giant spinning pyramid.

"Oh, my goodness. Look at that! Did you make that, Hedy?" Ana had never seen anything like it; she had no frame of reference for the design of it.

"No, that was all Darro. He made it, based on one a small one in the entry of the shop. It's modeled on a *Weihnachtspyramide*, a German Christmas pyramid. I'll show you a real one later. Amazing, huh?" Hedy was as proud of it as if she had made it herself.

"It's tremendous. And, nice that it moves everything slow enough that we can get the treats off easy enough," Mel piped up and grabbed one of the aprons that Hedy brought. It was a bright kelly green with red diamonds.

"Would you look at that, Willie? Would you like a cookie from here? I bet they have good cookies." A grandma had the hand of her grandson who appeared to be about three years old and was in awe, but also a little scared of the sights before him. He hovered close to her knee.

"Hi there, Willie. Did you know that anyone named Willie gets a free cookie today? I have gingerbread or sugar cookies or an iced chocolate Krampus cookie. What kind would you like?" Hedy bent toward the boy, who had his eyes fixed on the pyramid behind her.

"Choco," was his small reply. His grandma gave his hand a squeeze.

"He's a shy boy. He wouldn't sit on Santa's lap earlier today, just broke into tears."

"Oh, I understand. Here's a cookie for you, Willie. Don't worry about Santa. He will still bring you something nice." Hedy handed the cookie to Willie and his eyes lit up.

"Anything for Grandma?" Hedy saw the woman's eyes linger on the gingerbread.

"Yes, I'll take a dozen of the gingerbread to share with his parents. You have a wonderful display, by the way. And I love your costume." Hedy smiled to herself as Mel and Ana bagged up the order. The woman would be embarrassed if she knew this wasn't a costume.

"Enjoy the gingerbread. It is an authentic

*Pfeffernüsse* recipe from Germany. And here's our card, please come visit our shop on Griffin Avenue." Hedy swiped the woman's credit card on the small card reader she had bought for the market. It was amazing how you could go through life never actually handling cash.

"Thank you, I will. Come on, Willie. Let's go see what else we can find." She tugged at Willie's arm and he slowly followed, not wanting to take his eyes off the spinning pyramid, crumbs of chocolate Krampus on his face.

"So, you have a visitor, I hear," Ana spoke up once the pair were out of earshot.

"Yes, an inspector from the Concierge. She is here to investigate what happened up at the cabin. She wants to talk with you." Hedy watched a pair of elderly people smile and point at the pyramid, but they didn't approach.

"Yes, I received a call from someone, letting me know she wanted to meet with me. I told them I would come to Enumclaw since I was already planning to be here this weekend. It's weird that they even had my telephone number since it is a new one." Ana shrugged and then greeted a family that walked up to the booth.

"How is your cousin, Mel? Things back to normal?" Hedy could tell by Mel's expression that it wasn't.

"No, not at all. Things are worse, if that is possible. He is supposed to be grounded right now but he slipped out of the house after breakfast. I'm keeping an eye out for him or his little hell-raising friends. Honestly, I don't know what is going on with him." Mel tried to keep her voice low so the customers wouldn't hear but she was really worried about Dylan.

"I am sorry to hear that. I heard in passing that some shops had their windows broken. You don't suppose he was involved, do you?"

"Oh, I hope not. If he was involved, my uncle will go ballistic. Plus, how will he get into college with a juvie record? It's a nightmare." Mel brushed back the start of tears. She had to focus on what was happening right now and not think about all of that. Plus, she didn't want to ruin Ana's visit. There was time for tears later.

"What were you two talking about?" Ana turned back to them now that customers were gone.

"Oh nothing, just some family stuff. I'll fill you in later. Do you want to walk the market before it gets too busy? Hedy, do you mind?" Mel already knew the answer from Hedy's smile.

"Go, check it out. And keep your eye out for a booth for The Red Bat. That's where this dress came from. I want to check it out later."

Mel and Ana nodded and took off down the row, Mel not even taking off her apron. They were just so happy to be together, and it delighted Hedy to see it.

* * *

“Quite a big event, isn’t it?” Ana whispered into Mel’s ear to be heard above the din.

“Yes, it is a highlight of the year in town. Gives everybody a chance to buy some stuff from unusual shops from around the area. There should be carolers, some food wagons out back, and probably a strolling Santa Claus.” Mel gave Ana’s hand a squeeze, but she didn’t hold on to it. She still wasn’t sure about being very open of her feelings out in public. She wasn’t ashamed, she was just shy.

“All the focus on buying around Christmas baffles me. Why is the holiday all about what gifts you can get? I thought it was about celebrating the birth of Christ? All the talking snowmen, car ads with giant ribbons on top of them, and piles of presents seems at odds with that, no?” Ana wasn’t trying to be flippant; she really didn’t understand how all of it fit together.

“Different people celebrate it differently, but yes, it has become something of a time to show affection through the giving of gifts. People love presents, so I suppose it isn’t surprising that exchanging small gifts has become more with Black Friday and midnight sales and Santa’s big sleigh. Even with all that, Christmas is pretty cool. You’ll see.” Mel was determined to make Ana’s first Christmas amazing.

“There is that booth that Hedy was looking for, The Red Bat. That velvet dress is quite lovely.” Ana paused to touch the sleeve. She was certain she could never wear something so elegant, but it did look lovely on the mannequin.

"Pretty, isn't it? That would look so good on you. Although, we'd have to hem it, it is long." Mel chuckled and gave Ana a pat on the top of her head.

"Very funny, Mel. Yes, I'm short. And you are adorable. So, shut up." Ana gave Mel a quick kiss as they continued passed the booth.

* * *

The crowd continued to wax and wane, coming in spurts, but all stopped to marvel at the spinning Christmas pyramid. Sales were brisk; so much for the prediction of the rude lady earlier. Hedy was glad to see the pair of lovebirds return a while later so they could lend her a hand. At this pace, she would sell out of everything before the end of the market.

"Wow, quite a crowd, huh? No wonder with all the booths here. There are even vendors who have come in from other areas. We saw some really cool stuff for sale," Mel said as she slipped back behind the counter.

"Yes, I have never been to a Christmas market before, so it was interesting to see what it is all about." Ana perched on top of a tote container near the back, keeping out of the way.

"Well, a true Christmas market would look a bit different than this. You'd need to travel to Germany or Austria for the full experience. But it is nice to see little Enumclaw doing their part to share the experience, and it is nice for the vendors to make a little money."

"Hedy, why don't you go take a tour and check out that booth you wanted to see? It's almost directly across the hall from here. We saw a gorgeous green gown that Ana has her eye on. We can cover things here." Mel gave Ana a quick grin and was rewarded with a swift swipe at her leg.

"Thank you, I will. I'll only be a few minutes. I just restocked all the shelves, so what is left is all we have. I'm afraid we just might sell out." Hedy slid past Mel and exited the booth.

"Like that's a bad thing? More money, more money." Hedy and Mel laughed, and Ana came up to the counter to take Hedy's place. There were several customers lining up to get their treats, but Hedy didn't feel guilty; Mel could definitely handle it.

She walked the perimeter of the hall, past rows and rows of merchants in the middle of the hall that she could snake her way through. She wanted to make her way to Michael's booth first. Mel was right, it was almost directly across the hall, and she found it easily. He did have a mannequin dressed in green velvet, but he also had a large sign with the shop's name all lit in Christmas bulbs. He was right that it would have been impossible to miss.

"Well, this is quite a display." Hedy walked up as a customer was leaving with her bag, clearly pleased with her purchase. He had brought just a sampling of the store's wares, but the two rolling racks were jammed packed, though still meticulously organized and color coordinated.

"Yes, I didn't think subtle was the right approach for this event. So far, sales have been good. I wasn't sure what to expect. Vintage clothing usually has a limited market, but everyone must be in a buying mood. I should have brought more jewelry; that seems to be the biggest hit." Michael's voice sounded amazed to Hedy, like he was genuinely surprised people were buying his things.

"Well, I am glad that things are going well. We are selling well, too. Although, cookies at Christmas is almost a gimme. A little hard to sell in January, when everyone starts their diet," Hedy said dryly. Michael laughed and his curls shook.

"Yes, I would suspect that is the one month when your shop struggles. But right after that you have Valentine's Day, so you are saved. You should take a January vacation and hit a beach somewhere. I have some lovely one-piece suits back at the shop you could try on." He smiled devilishly. Clearly, he was always trying to make a sale, but Hedy wondered if he was flirting as well.

"Oh, I will have things to occupy my time, never fear. But on a serious note, I hear there was some vandalism near your shop. What happened, do you know?"

Before Michael could answer, a customer came up to purchase a pair of red leather gloves. Rather than hover, Hedy took a few moments to browse through the rack until he finished his sale.

"Yes, it was awful. The whole street and sidewalk had glass everywhere. Someone came through and smashed most of the shop windows. They grabbed things out of the displays, but it doesn't look like they entered the buildings. Whoever it was seemed more interested in destruction than actual looting. Just terrible." Michael's voice had a hard edge to it.

"But they didn't hit your shop?"

"No, thank goodness. I managed to avoid the smash and grab. I chalk it up to my Irish luck. Oh, and the magic spells of course." Michael smiled that devilish grin again and Hedy honestly couldn't tell whether he was joking or not.

"Well, I am glad you missed being a target, no matter the reason. I feel so badly for the shops near you. I had met the owner of the store next to yours, I think her name is Kaitlyn, and I can't imagine how upset she is today."

"She's here. No doubt some sales can help offset the loss. Her store has plywood over the window right now until the glazier can come to put in the new window on Monday. I just hope the police find the people responsible. Can't let something like that go, they will only escalate." Michael turned to greet another customer, and Hedy decided to leave him to it. She gave him a wave and took off to finish the loop around the hall.

The crowd had definitely thickened. The market was in full swing and Hedy could hear the Christmas carolers working on their version of We Three Kings from somewhere in the center of the hall. Most people had bags in hand, and she was glad to see it; small shops had a hard time competing with big retail stores or online sales.

The noise of the hall increased but not all of it sounded pleasant. There was an undercurrent of shouting and Hedy realized it was getting louder the closer she got to her side of the hall. She picked up her pace when she saw one of the booths near her had merchandise scattered all over the cement floor.

"There are four of them. In masks. Try to cut them off!" she heard a security guard yell to another who darted toward the middle of the hall, no doubt trying to reach the opening at the far end that led to the beer garden and food trucks.

Hedy heard Mel yell and she started to run. She was only a few booths away, but she could see figures in sweatshirts fleeing and her tiered stands on the ground, smashed. She saw the last figure grab the top of the pyramid and give it a hard pull. The whole thing toppled over into three large pieces before Ana and Mel could stop it.

# CHAPTER TWENTY

Hedy, I am so sorry! He was so fast. He just jumped on the first tier and then yanked before we could stop him." Mel was in tears, trying to pick up the remains of the cookies as if they could be salvaged. Ana was trying to push the parts of the pyramid out of the way, but they were a bit too heavy for her.

"Mel, it isn't your fault. I saw what happened. Don't bother trying to pick those cookies up. We'll just get a broom." Hedy was looking down the hall as she spoke, watching the crowd to see if the kid was still there. People were heading out the back entrance, so she assumed the vandal headed that way.

"It was definitely a kid. They didn't say a word though. Not even laughing or swearing, not anything." Mel's voice grew louder and more upset. She knew it wasn't her fault, yet she felt responsible in some way. Maybe if she had seen the kid approach instead of talking with Ana, or maybe if she has tried to grab onto an arm, she might have been able to stop the whole disaster.

"Mel, don't blame yourself. The child came out of nowhere. There was nothing we could have done to stop what happened." Ana squatted down by Mel and gently pulled her to her feet. There were broken Krampus cookies all around them on the floor. The irony wasn't lost on Hedy and she laughed.

"What? Why are you laughing?" Mel watched Hedy go from chuckling to full on belly laugh and she couldn't understand why.

"Look down. Look at your feet." Hedy could barely speak the words. "Krampus."

It took Mel a minute but then she understood, and she started laughing too, more at Hedy's hysteria than anything else. Yes, it was funny that Krampus cookies should be smashed by the very kid that Krampus would have snatched up in his bag. Anahita looked at both of them like they were crazy.

"Okay, enough of this," Hedy said as she wiped the tears from her eyes and regained her composure. "Mel, can you call Darro and ask him to come back early? He can help us tear down the booth and then we can go back to the house. I'd like to put this day behind me. There is a glass of whiskey with my name on it at home."

"I wonder if they caught the kid? They had on some kind of Halloween masks and were dressed in black. Should be easy to spot among all the red and green," Ana said. She briefly thought about following the crowd outside to see what was happening, but she decided Mel needed her nearby. Mel's loyalty and sense of duty were one of the things Ana loved about her, even if she did end up taking things too personally sometimes.

"I hope it wasn't Dylan." Mel sounded serious again, thinking about her cousin.

"Oh, it probably wasn't him. You would have recognized him, no doubt, even with the mask. Let's not borrow trouble," Ana advised. The crowd was milling by, observing the scene and making comments as they went. This wasn't how Hedy wanted to get the word out about the shop. The quicker they cleaned up and left the market, the better.

"I'll call Darro. Then, I'll call my uncle and see if Dylan has shown up." Mel started scrolling through her contacts, looking for Darro's number. She had a terrible feeling that Dylan was involved.

"Is everyone alright over here?" Michael arrived from among the crowd, looking concerned and shaking his head at the mess.

"Yes, we are fine, unlike our poor cookies. Good thing you got one when you did. We're finished here for the day." Hedy hoped she didn't look as exasperated as she felt. She was trying hard to keep her composure.

"What a shame. Damn hooligan, I hear. Probably one of the ones who smashed the windows yesterday. I hope the police find them. What can I do to help?" Michael's clothing was far too nice to be hauling out the wooden pyramid and cookie shambles.

"Oh, we appreciate the offer, but our friend Darro is on his way to help. He has the truck to load all this out. We'll sweep it up with a broom and be done with it all. Thanks, though. You better get back to your stall before something gets stolen." Hedy appreciated his willingness to help her out and she did her best to give him a good smile. She would be mortified if she knew it looked more like a grimace.

"I asked a very nice lady to mind the stall for me, and unless she is helping herself to the scarves, I think I am alright. But if you have things in hand, I'll head back. I'll swing by your store tomorrow, if that is alright, to see how things are going. Maybe by then there will be news of an arrest and you can be picking out the villain in a line up." Michael chuckled and Hedy gamely tried to join him. The idea that it might be Mel's cousin behind all this took the mirth out of his joking.

"Thanks, Michael. I look forward to your visit." She gave him a wave as he headed off. Mel was off the phone with Darro and looking puzzled.

"Who was that, Hedy?"

"That is Michael, the owner of The Red Bat, that shop in town you told me to check out. He is very nice and that's where I picked up this dress. He's coming by the shop tomorrow to check on things." Hedy turned from watching him walk away to see the concerned look on Ana's face.

"You know he isn't mortal, Hedy. Has he told you that?" Ana asked, looking from the startled faces of Mel and Hedy and realizing she was spilling secrets.

"What? What are you talking about?" Hedy stepped closer to the girls so that no one in the crowd would overhear them.

"I can't tell you exactly what he is, but I can tell you he isn't human. As an elemental, I can sense another who is not...well, pardon the term, but not mundane like humans. Those with powers and abilities give off a scent that is unmistakable to undines. Humans smell different. Not bad, mind you, just different." She saw the worried look on Mel's face and wanted to reassure her.

"I don't know anything about that. The most he has ever said was a joke that the vandals didn't smash up his shop because of the magic spell he had on the building. Are you sure, Ana?" Hedy felt a knot in her stomach starting to grow.

"Yes, I am afraid so. Your friend is definitely not a human. That might not be a bad thing, but you should know what you are dealing with." Ana was sorry to be the one bearing the news; Hedy's face looked like someone had just poured cold water all over her.

"Well, that's a situation for another day. Tonight is about getting the pyramid cleaned up and getting back to the shop. Hopefully Darro is on his way." Hedy really didn't think she could take one more thing going wrong today. The sooner she could get home, the sooner she could put this day behind her.

"He should be here any time; he lives just a few miles from here." Mel was trying to be helpful, but she could see it wasn't having much effect. She glanced helplessly over at Ana and two exchanged a silent conversation.

"I guess on the bright side it means you will get your meeting with Miss Vaduva sooner than we thought, Ana. At least you can get that over with and she can be on her way. She is an interesting woman, to put it mildly." Hedy gave Ana a weak smile and perched on one of the large rubber totes behind the table as a makeshift stool.

"Why does she want to talk with me? I'm sure she knows everything that happened with Lyssa." Ana had found the call from the Concierge cryptic, with little detail as to why anyone would want to meet with her.

"She said she needs to hear from you what your experience was. She is deciding if I am fit to continue hosting a waystation. Apparently endangering the lives of my guests is frowned upon." Hedy chuckled in a gallows humor sort of way. It wasn't anything she hadn't thought about herself; she couldn't very well blame the Concierge from thinking it, too.

"That's nonsense. Bren and I both wouldn't hear of leaving, even when you asked us to. We were there of our own free will, and I will tell Miss Vaduva that in person. You did nothing wrong, and in fact, without your help, those women would have been more traumatized than they already were by that awful man, Mr. Jeffries." Ana was getting worked up just thinking about it all and how unfair it was that Hedy should be taking any blame.

"I appreciate that, Ana, I really do. But you must promise me that whatever the investigator asks you, you will answer her honestly. If it is better that I no longer host guests, I would have to abide by that decision, as much as I would hate that." Hedy stood up at the sight of Darro approaching and before she could start to cry. Saying it out loud made the possibility all the more real and she couldn't imagine losing her waystation.

"What in the bloody hell happened here?" Darro's voice came out like a roar, startling the shoppers that were still lingering near the wreckage of the stall. He gave the dolly a sharp push before standing it upright.

"Someone thought it would be a good idea to pull it down, destroying everything. Looked like a kid in a Halloween mask. They ran off before anyone caught them." Hedy sounded tired as she gave Darro the abbreviated story. "If we can just pack up everything and head back to the house, I would be really grateful."

"Sure thing. But we need to fetch a broom and a garbage pail from someone. Perhaps the lasses can help with that while I start loading out the wood?" Darro watched both Ana and Mel jump forward and head toward the front of the hall. "Why don't you follow me out to the truck and take a wee rest while we get this all cleaned up?"

"I'd rather help, and then we can all head back quickly. I am so sorry all your work ended up toppled over. Hopefully it can be fixed to use again?" Hedy watched as Darro picked up the smashed motor and the splintered paddles from the top of the pyramid.

"Oh aye, it can be, if need be. I suspect you won't have need of such a whirlygig for a while, though. If we need to rebuild her, it won't take much time. I am just sorry to see all those good treats go to waste on the floor. All for some rumpus." Darro practically spat out the last words. He was getting his dander up just thinking about some brat causing all this mischief.

"Well at least we made quite a few sales before all this happened, so the day isn't a total loss. Looks like the girls are back with the broom."

Tearing down the display took less time than setting it up and it wasn't long before they had everything loaded back up in the truck. Ana and Mel had been dropped off at the hall by Mel's mom but luckily there was just enough room in the back of Darro's truck for them and the drive was a short one. Too long in the back of the pickup would have been uncomfortably cold for the girls, pressed up against the wooden slats of the pyramid.

Hedy and Darro rode in silence back toward

the house. They pulled up to the curb and Darro waved them all off from helping to unload the truck. He could manage it very well himself.

"You two must be chilled from that ride. Come on, let's get inside and I'll get you some tea." Hedy pulled out her key for the front door, but latch turned easily. Maybe Yami went out and left it unlocked?

She knew right away that no one was in the house; you can just tell when a house is empty, even before you shout out for anyone to answer. Hedy peered into the shop, and though the lights were still on and Raluca's book was still on the table, she knew she wasn't there.

"That's odd. I wonder where she went? I thought she was going to stay here and wait for Ana." Hedy walked over to the table and picked up the book. The cover felt smooth in her hands and the image of Raluca and Yami leaving together flashed before her, a look of distaste and annoyance on Raluca's face.

Where would they go together? And why was she seeing this image?

"Hedy, what is wrong? You look like you are freaked out." Mel came up to her and touched her softly on the arm. Hedy could feel the touch, but she could still see Raluca and Yami in her mind. She saw them leave the house and get into Hedy's car, taking off at high speed. How was she seeing this?

"Something is wrong. Yami and Raluca are together in my car but I don't think Raluca left willingly. I think Yami took her."

# CHAPTER TWENTY-ONE

"I've never had the pleasure of meeting a Moroaica before. You must pardon my appearance. I haven't quite been myself since that little encounter with the intrepid baker."

The voice came from the darkness at the back of the cave. Raluca and Yami had made their way into the forest and to the dark little cave where even Raluca's keen eyes were having a hard time adjusting to the darkness. She could just make out the shape of a darker figure melting into the shadows.

"All this drama is hardly necessary. If you have something to say, there is no need to drag me into the dirt and the woods. Do you know how hard it is to get sap out of wool? Ridiculous." Raluca really didn't care about the wear on her Chanel jacket; she was more interested to see what the voice would say to such goading. She felt Yami's hand tighten uncomfortably on her thin arm.

"Oh, I do apologize for the drama, as you say. And bringing someone as august as you to a dirty cave in the woods is likely the height of offense. But in my current state, it really was necessary. You see, our friend the baker caused me quite a grave injury and it takes quite a bit out of me to leave the safety of this cave. I have had to rely on my crows and, of course, Miss Hayashi. She has been quite useful. Thank you, my dear."

The voice was calm and cool, with just the slightest rasp indicating it was taking effort to speak. Raluca could make out a faint orange glow coming from deep within the cave and she guessed it was this glow that kept the speaker nearby.

"Let's get on with this, shall we? I am an old woman and I have neither the time nor the patience for this. Ask what you want to know and let's be done with it." Again, she felt Yami's hand on her arm as the woman pulled her to a flat top stone that served as a seat. With minimum force, she felt Yami pull her down to a sitting position.

"As you say, let's begin. The opportunity to learn the location of every waystation in the network is one that I can hardly pass up. It won't be much longer before my strength is restored and when it is, I will take great pleasure in visiting each and every waystation along the network. And you will tell me where they are."

Raluca watched as the dark figure came a bit closer, inching toward the dim light. She could make out reddish hair and dark eyes in a face but everything else was blackness.

"Why do you think I would help you in any

way? It's laughable that you think by merely asking, I will provide you information that we keep separate and secret for just this reason." Raluca gave a dry laugh and it reverberated in the cave. Yami said nothing next to her.

"Naturally, I didn't expect you to give me the information willingly. But I do expect you to give it to me. Miss Hayashi is quite persuasive. It is one of her many talents. In addition to being a kitsune, as you no doubt guessed, she is also highly skilled at finding just the right pressure point to illicit a desired response. Isn't that right, my dear?" Lyssa's voice had her usual light and easy tone but the malice under the surface was inescapable.

"I do what is required. Nothing more. Nothing less," Yami said simply, directing her words at no one in particular. She did not care for this part of the job, but it often was part of why she was hired. She did what others often wouldn't or couldn't do.

"You may find me a bit different from your usual interrogation. The Vaduvas are made of stern stuff. I don't expect you to believe me, but as I said, let's get this over with." Raluca spoke with almost a wistfulness to her voice and it surprised Yami. It wasn't the usual reaction from someone about to be tortured.

"Very well. Let's see if Miss Hayashi has any tricks up her sleeve that might be...inspiring for you."

Lyssa stepped closer again and Raluca saw a face that looked like a mask of horror. It was aged, like wet layers of husks that had been torn and puckered, with a slash for a mouth. Apparently, this is what an ancient goddess with a mortal wound looked like.

"Get on with it, girl." Raluca's voice bounced hard against the stone walls, followed by a deep breath.

# CHAPTER TWENTY-TWO

"Hedy, why do you think Yami took Raluca? What's going on?"

Hedy knew Ana was speaking but she was still seeing the images of Raluca and Yami in her car, driving out of town, in her mind. Where were they going? How was she seeing this?

"Hedy. Hedy!" Ana's voice cut through the vision and Hedy snapped back into the shop, looking at the worried faces staring at her.

"I...I don't know. I just know that something has happened. Somehow, I can see what is happening in my mind, like I am seeing my own memory. I saw Yami and Raluca in my car, heading north out of town." Hedy felt like she was caught between two worlds, one foot in her shop and one in the vision in her mind. It was disorienting and frightening, like she might fall down and there would be no floor to catch her. She grasped the chair at Raluca's table and vision swallowed her mind in a wave.

"Where are they going, can you tell?" She heard

Mel's voice but it sounded far away. Hedy watched the vision for a minute, trying to tell what road they were traveling on. It all looked very familiar.

"They are on a windy road, past pastures, and there is a sign up ahead. It is a white sign, red letters and a green shape on it. It is coming closer... the Christmas tree farm." Hedy saw them drive past the farm, but then turn on a side road just behind it. Hedy's vision flooded with a wave of red and pain engulfed her mind. She screamed out, crumpling into the chair.

"Hedy! What happened? Are you alright?" Mel's panicked voice was floating above her but all Hedy could see was the red that now filled her eyes. The pain radiated from behind her eyeballs and traveled down every nerve in her body.

"Stop, oh, please stop. No, they are torturing her!" Hedy's face was a mask of pain, her eyes rolling back into her head. Mel grasped her face, trying to bring her out of it.

"Ana, help me!" Mel didn't know what to do, Hedy was writhing and lashing in the chair, moaning as if her own flesh were being burned or cut. How could they stop this? Mel's heartbeat thumped in her ears. The sweat from her palms was slick on Hedy's cheeks.

"Mel, we have to sever the connection somehow. Take the book from her hands." Ana was pulling Hedy out of the chair, away from anything that Raluca might have touched. Hedy was bigger than Ana and it took all her strength to pull her up and away, getting her into another seat nearby. "Get me a big bowl of water, Mel. Cool water."

Ana had no idea if this would work but she didn't know what else to do. Something was connecting Hedy to Raluca and unless they could break that connection, Hedy would feel everything that she was feeling. Hedy screamed again, lashing her arms blindly as if she could stop whatever was happening to Raluca.

Mel took a big metal bowl from Hedy's work counter and dumped out the ripe pears that it was holding. She hurriedly filled the bowl from the tap, unsure as to how much water Ana needed. She ran the bowl over to Ana, slopping the water on the wooden floor as she went.

"Thanks, Mel. Help me get her hands into the water. Hold them under." Mel stood behind Hedy, grasping her wrists and using every bit of strength she had to plunge her hands into the water. Hedy was moaning, straining against Mel's efforts to hold her. Mel looked up at Ana's face, opening her mouth to speak. She saw Ana's eyes close and heard a low murmur from her lips, so Mel kept quiet and concentrated on holding Hedy's hands where they were.

Ana's hands were in the water, undulating back and forth, caressing the water and letting it filter through her fingertips. In her mind, she focused every bit of her energy and thought into the water itself, down to the molecules as they swirled within the bowl. The water had an energy and

Ana's hands were amplifying it, directing the energy to swirl and roll against the metal sides. The water was frothing, close to breaching the edge of the bowl but Ana kept it contained, focused on just the small container and the pair of hands within it.

Mel held Hedy rigidly, locking her arms so that Hedy couldn't pull her hands free. She noticed that the moans from Hedy were growing softer and her hands weren't thrashing as hard as they were before. Hedy's breath began to flow from a ragged gasp to more of a forced in and out, as if the pain was receding. Mel felt Hedy's body begin to relax against her. She still held tight, just in case she tried to break free.

After a few more moments, Ana was silent, and the water began to still. Mel could see that she had placed her hands on top of Hedy's; all three of them were touching now. The water swirled around them for a few more moments and then it was still.

"Hedy?" Mel was afraid to break the silence, but the woman was starting to stir against her arms. Hedy gave a large exhalation.

"Mel? Ana?" Her voice was weak. Her eyes flickered open, blinking at the light.

"Yes, we are here, Hedy. Are you alright?" Ana's voice poured over Hedy and she took another huge breath. She felt a twinge of fire on every nerve, like a little shock wave after a tsunami.

"Why are you holding me in water?" Hedy

looked at her hands, still plunged in the bowl with Mel and Ana holding her there. The girls slowly released her and pulled out their own hands. Her wrists ached from Mel's hard grip.

"Let me get you a towel." Mel hurried over to the counter and brought back a few hand towels. Hedy slowly pulled her hands from the bowl.

"Hedy, do you remember anything?" Ana spoke again with all the calmness of a mountain pond.

"I saw a vision, of Yami and Raluca, and then everything went red and this pain draped over me." She didn't dare speak anymore in case it came back.

"We had to break the connection. Ana thought the water would help and it did." Mel said, proudly smiling at Ana and her ingenuity. Ana smiled back.

"What I want to know is how you had the connection with Raluca in the first place. It couldn't have just come from holding that book." Ana took the bowl from the table and placed it carefully on the counter, trying not to spill any more water. She dropped the hand towel on the floor and used her foot to wipe away some of the spills.

"Raluca took energy from me earlier, drawing it out of me because she was weak. She's a Moroica and she feeds on energy. She said we might have a connection for a bit afterward." Hedy's head was pounding, but this time the pain was her own. She had a massive headache right behind her eyes and she needed some aspirin.

"Then you were not only seeing what happened to her, but you were feeling whatever it is that Yami is or was doing to her." Mel gave Ana a worried look. What if the connection came back?

"We have to find her. If Yami is torturing her, this could very well kill her. She is an old woman." Hedy stood up shakily and Mel instinctively grabbed her arm to support her. "I'm okay, I just need some aspirin. Can you get Darro? We need a ride out to the Christmas tree farm. They are just past there."

Hedy watched Mel run to the door and shout for Darro, her mind still whirling. She was back in the present moment, in the shop with Ana and Mel, but the fear that she would be drawn back into Raluca's mind was palpable. She couldn't imagine what was happening to the old woman and how she was bearing it. She also couldn't imagine what they could do to help her once they made it to the farm. If Bren were here, at least they would have his fire as back up. But Bren was gone. They were on their own..

"Hedy, what will we do when we find them? Do you have a plan?" Ana must have been thinking the same thing as Hedy, because doubt was etched on her face. Worse yet, she was looking to Hedy for answers and she didn't have any.

"I'm not sure," Hedy confessed. "Yami has Raluca and I don't know who or what Yami might be. I suspect Lyssa is behind it all and is likely there, too. I'm hoping we have the advantage of numbers and maybe we can help Raluca free herself. It's times like this that I wish I were more like my guests; I feel useless as a powerless human."

She gave Ana a weak smile, but she was quite serious. Being involved with those who had powers left her feeling unprotected and weak.

"Any more magical weapons in your collection? There is always that elfish knife." Ana looked toward the entry.

"I have Aaron Burr's revolver, the one that shot Hamilton, but I doubt it still works and there is nothing magical about that. There is the knife, but I can't imagine that Lyssa would let anyone get close enough to her for that to be effective again. She's too smart for that. No, I don't think the collection is going to be any help this time." Hedy felt a panic in the pit of her stomach. Maybe going to save Raluca was going to get them all killed.

"Well, maybe we need to find out just what kind of being your friend, Michael, really is. He might have some power that can help."

Hedy flinched. She wasn't at all prepared to find out what the story was with Michael and nevermind how strange it would be to ask him. She barely knew him.

"Darro is coming now. Are we going to head out there?" Mel was back in the shop, her face ruddy from running outside to get Darro.

"Yes. We have to do something to save Raluca. You two don't have to come, of course. I'd be lying if I said I wasn't more than a little afraid of how this thing is going to go down." Mel's phone rang, interrupting Hedy.

"It's my uncle. I better answer." Mel swiped the screen and said hello quickly into the phone. Her face instantly looked worried. "What? Are you sure it was him? Where?"

Mel's mouth was a hard slash and Ana instinct-ively put a hand on her arm.

"OK, I'm heading out. I'll call you." Mel swiped the screen again and looked at both Ana and Hedy. "My uncle says that Dylan was one of the kids at the Christmas market and he helped steal a car. The kids were driving north, out of town. My uncle is going to go looking for them."

"Is it possible they are heading toward the Christmas tree farm?" Hedy felt the panic rising into her throat; there was no way that all this was just a coincidence.

"We're going to find out. I have to go find Dylan."

# CHAPTER TWENTY-THREE

The old woman was remarkably resilient. Yami had a rather eclectic skill set that would induce pain in a number of places - digits, limbs, eyes, mind - but Raluca was stoic throughout. The cave echoed occasionally with a small cry or a grunt escaping through clenched teeth, but beyond that, it was quiet, and Lyssa was growing impatient.

"This is your speciality, no? What is the delay?" Lyssa's irritation was clear in her voice; if she could have done the job herself, she would have. Her physical strength wasn't up to the challenge at the moment, despite the presence of the stone.

"She is resistant. She is unlike others I have persuaded." Yami didn't want to use the word 'torture' but she knew that is what this was. It was usually an effective and quick method to gain what her employers wanted. She wasn't fond of it but, as with some chores, sometimes you just have to grit your teeth and get to work. Raluca was proving problematic, though.

"Ha, I told you I wouldn't be as easy as you hoped. Your crude methods lack any of the finesse of the early days." Raluca turned her head to spit a small globule of blood before looking back at her captors.

"If she isn't going to cooperate. I suppose there is no reason to keep her alive. As much as knowing the location of all the waystations would be useful to me, I can still journey on without them. Or perhaps, one of her employees would be more malleable." Lyssa's voice still sounded strained but there was the return of a lilt, as if she were considering asking them over for tea. Yami found it rather chilling, and apparently so did Raluca because she began to shift on her perch.

"'Anger is an acid that can do more harm to the vessel in which it is stored than on anything on which it is poured.' Surely, you remember the ancient philosopher, Seneca? What do you hope to gain from all this? Even if I told you the location of the waystations, even if you somehow managed to visit them or destroy them, what does that gain you? It's not as if they can't rebuild. You can't kill the idea of the waystations." Raluca was speaking to Lyssa but she kept her eyes on Yami.

"Destroying the waystations would release chaos into each city, each community, and that is enough. Let them rebuild. I will just destroy them again. Once I have my strength back, time is not a factor, Miss Vaduva. Save yourself from any further unpleasantness and just tell me what I want to know."

"What you cannot understand is the role the waystations have played in human history. The sanctuary they have been for those, like Miss Hayashi and her family. Whatever your mad scheme is, there is no reason to involve the waystations." Raluca's eyes were piercing into Yami's face, as if she could will her to understand the gravity of the situation.

"What do you mean my family?" Yami asked before Lyssa could speak again.

"We served as a haven for your grandmother. Did you not know that?" Raluca tried to keep her voice even but it was vital that she get the kitsune on her side.

"My father's family has lived in Okinawa for generations. There is no waystation there," Yami said flatly.

"Your maternal grandmother. In 1942, your grandmother - I believe her name was Emiko, was it not? She lived in San Francisco with her family. Her parents had emigrated from Japan before the United States banned Japanese immigration in the 1920s. The benefits of a long memory, no?" Raluca spoke casually, trying not to rush the story. She needed to reel in the woman.

"Enough history, Miss Vadu-" Yami stopped Lyssa with a raise of her hand.

"Let her finish, please. What of my grandmother?" Yami watched the old woman's face intently, her fists were clenched at her side.

"Emiko was a modern girl in 1942, with a sweetheart and the bright future of youth when the United States decided to intern all residents of Japanese ancestry. Her parents and her brother were swept up, but Emiko wasn't home that day. She had been secretly meeting her sweetheart. Once she learned of their fate, she fled to the safety of the San Francisco waystation. She lived there, in hiding, for four years. Without the waystation, your grandmother would have suffered the fate of her parents and brother. Without the waystation, you would not exist, Miss Hayashi."

Raluca's voice was fading. She didn't have much energy left; it had taken all her will to survive the torture. If she did not convinced the young kitsune to stop, she knew she wouldn't be able to hold out.

"My Obaasan never spoke of her youth. My mother knew she had lived in this country for a time, but she refused to discuss it," Yami said, her mind clearly not in the present moment as she spoke.

"Enough. This is a ploy. Do not fall for her Moroi tricks. Let us finish this." Lyssa moved closer to Yami as she spoke.

"Search your heart, kitsune. You know this to be true." Raluca had no more words and barely enough breath to speak.

"The postcard…from the San Francisco World's Fair in 1939. It was one of the few things my grandmother had in a small jewel box that my mother received when she died. We never knew how she came by it or what it meant to her."

Yami stepped away from Lyssa and came behind Raluca, reaching for the old woman's hands that were tightly bound. She used the knife, still wet with Raluca's blood, to cut the cord.

"No, what are you doing? You must not fall for this trickery. She is using sympathy to escape. Do not be fooled." Panic crept into Lyssa's voice. She didn't have the strength to fight the kitsune. The wound in her side throbbed as if she needed a reminder that her strength would fail her.

"Enough. I am done. This is over. Whether the story is true or not, I do not want to be a part of this. I will refund your payment, and I am returning to Tokyo. I am taking the old woman out of here." Yami began to carefully lift Raluca from the stone seat and she could feel the old woman's weight in her arms.

"This ends tonight. Go if you must, but leave the Moroica to me. She is nothing to you." Lyssa moved to put herself between the entrance of the cave and the kitsune.

"As I said, the old woman leaves with me. Do not make me harm you. I will if I must."

"Your knife is not the one the baker used, kitsune. It has no magical properties. You have nothing that can harm me."

Lyssa sounded bold but Yami knew there was fear behind her words. If the demigoddess were really that invulnerable, she would not sound so desperate. “Perhaps that is true. But, as you know, I have very sharp teeth in my true form and the bite of a kitsune may have magic enough to end you. Shall we find out?” Yami took a step closer, keeping Raluca close to her side. They were leaving together, no matter what it took.

“This isn’t over, Kitsune. We have a score to settle.” Lyssa hissed and the cloak of black around her began to shimmer and then swirl, like smoke on the wind. In the dark of the cave, Yami could barely see that the dark form was gone and not just pressed into the shadows.

“Let’s go. Can you walk?” Yami felt the old woman take a few steps in reply. She used her strength to bolster Raluca, holding her tight against her body as a support. “Can you draw energy from me?” Yami saw a slight shake of Raluca’s head in reply. Apparently a moroi could not draw strength from a being such as Yami.

The pair walked slowly toward the dark light at the front of the cave. Yami wondered if the old woman would even make it back to the car, parked at the Christmas tree farm. There was no one to ask for help so Yami would have to support the old woman through the dark path and hope that she had enough strength to survive.

“Wait. Crystal…” The old woman stopped in her tracks, as if gathering her energy to speak.

“The crystal? The one in the cave? What of it?” Yami found a stone near the cave entrance and gently placed Raluca down on it. She watched the old woman gulp air several times before speaking again.

"We must bring it. It cannot remain. You must get it."

"Why? Let's just get you out of here."

"No, we can't. Lyssa. The crystal." The old woman fell silent again, breathing heavy in the darkening light.

"Alright, you sit here. I will figure out how to get it out. I believe that it is embedded in stone but maybe if I change form, I can dig it out."

Yami walked back into the cave and trained her eyes on the dim orange glow at the far end before her. Every cell in her body was telling her to turn around and stay away from the crystal. It seemed to radiate that it did not wish to be disturbed, but Yami forced her feet forward until she was at the center of the orange glow. She began to remove her clothing.

# CHAPTER TWENTY-FOUR

Darro was rumbling along the road out of town, pushing the pedal on the old Ford truck as far as it would go. Hedy worried that Mel and Ana would freeze in the back of the truck, but they were bundled up in thick coats and a blanket from the house. The cold was the least of their problems and everyone knew it. No doubt what was waiting at the Christmas tree farm was far more dangerous than a little wind-chill.

"So, we think your guest, this Yami woman, took the old gal to the tree lot? Why would she do that?" Darro kept looking over at Hedy as he spoke, and she really wished he would keep his eyes on the darkening road. It was dusk, the hour when deer would likely jump out.

"I don't know why she took her, but I suspect it has something to do with Lyssa, who may not be gone after all. I could be wrong but why else would Yami kidnap Raluca and take her out of town? There has to be a connection." Hedy braced herself as the Ford bucked along, and she felt awful for the girls in the back, perched on the metal bed of the truck.

"And all this has something to do with those hellions who tore down the pyramid? What do they have to do with anything? One of them is Mel's cousin?" Darro was trying his best to piece it all together but clearly there was information missing.

"We know that Dylan and his friends stole a car at the Christmas market, and they were headed out of town toward the tree farm. We know that Yami took Raluca and they are near the tree farm as well. We don't know the connection but there has to be one. We also don't know what we are up against once we get there." Hedy knew they had to go to the farm to help but she felt totally unprepared for what they might face, and it frightened her.

"If Skinny Malinky Longlegs were here, our man Bren, that would at least be something. I don't mind a fair fight, but I don't like goin' in t'something blind as a garden mole. Still and all, I've got a metal bat in the back of the truck and that should go a long way to helping to calm everyone's nerves." The truck rumbled on and Hedy didn't answer. She had no idea whether a physical weapon would be enough to stop whatever was happening to Raluca, but it was the best they had at the moment. Darro was right; having Bren with them would have been a huge help.

Darro found the farm but it was closed - everyone was supposed to be at the Christmas market. Luckily, the rusting metal gate that closed off the parking lot wasn't locked. Two other cars had discovered the same thing: Hedy's Corvair and a black Honda.

Darro had barely stopped the truck before Mel bounded out the back of the truck bed, tossing the blanket off to one side. She slipped the hood of her parka down and started running toward the tree farm barn, with Ana close on her heels.

"Mel, wait. We need a plan. We can't just race in without knowing what we are doing." Hedy tried to catch them, but they were far ahead. She heard a loud whomping bellow from behind her and it caused all three women to stop and turn. It was Darro.

"Oy, let's gather up. We only have numbers on our side, so let's not lose that advantage, shall we? Mel, take this crowbar. Ana, I have a piece of 2x4 for you. Hedy, take these lopping shears." Darro and Hedy caught up to the girls and Darro passed out his weapons. Hedy had no idea how she would use lopping shears to stop anyone and she felt foolish for even holding them. Still, it was the best they had.

"I'm not using a crowbar on Dylan. I'm going to talk to him and make him understand." Mel tried to hand back the crowbar to Darro but he shook his head.

"I'm not suggesting that you do. But if that

Lyssa creature is in there, we might need something more than words. Unless any of you have a better idea?" Darro look at each of them in turn but no one said anything. "Fine. Let's take these with us then, just in case. How many kids are in this gang, do we think?" Darro started walking toward the barn, but at a much more deliberate pace.

"I would guess four or five kids. Promise me you won't hurt them, Darro." Mel couldn't imagine facing her uncle if anything she did injured Dylan.

"I have no intention of hurting anyone. I promise you that. If someone attacks me, I canna swear they won't get some scratches in the effort, but I'll do my best to avoid hurting anyone. I didn't start this party, remember that. They did." Darro reached the small gate near the path leading toward the barn and it swung open easily. Someone had already broken the padlock.

There were lights on the outside of the barn, lighting up the area around it and making it easy to see that there was no one right in front of them. The sky was dark but not pitch black just yet, except for a small patch of darkness that seemed to be moving from the east. The patch was undulating, and the sound of crows began to swell.

Hedy had never seen so many crows is one group; she had never actually seen them fly in any kind of formation before. The crows were swooping down, heading toward the field of cut trees just beyond the lights from the barn.

"What in blazes is that? Crows?" Darro could barely be heard over the noise of them. "There must be five hundred of them, at least."

"What's bringing them here?" Ana soft voice could only be heard by Hedy, who was standing next to her.

"Lyssa. She must have called them here." Hedy felt the truth of it as she said it. There was no way this was anything other than Lyssa's doing.

From the barn, a few figures ran out, heading also toward the field. They were running so fast that all Hedy saw was a blur of plaid coats. A few moments later, the strands of Christmas tree lights blazed on and the area around the cut trees was washed with light. Thousands of bulbs blazed into the night, pouring down on the crows that perched on boughs and fence posts. The crows had gone silent.

"Dylan! Dylan, is that you?" Mel cried out toward one of the running figures and she bolted after it. Ana tried to grab her arm, but she was too fast.

"Dylan! Is that you?" a voice cried back at her, in a taunting sing song fashion before breaking into laughter. It was a girl's voice.

"Dylan, it's Mel. Where are you?" Mel kept running, careful to avoid the trees along the path as she navigated toward the center of the field. With all these cut trees, the kids could be hiding anywhere.

"Dylan, Dylan, Dylan..." The girls voice continued to repeat her but now another voice joined it, a male voice. They were taunting her.

"Enough of this rubbish. Come out you scoundrels. We mean business." Darro's voice roared into the night, breaking the sound of the kids' chant. It was silent for a moment and then two figures emerged from behind the trees. Mel thought she recognized Dylan's friend, Randy. She didn't recognize the girl.

"Randy, where's Dylan?" Mel tried to move closer to the pair, but Darro's large arm blocked her way. He wanted to keep them at arm's distance.

"He's here. So is Steve, and so is Harley. We are all here." Randy sounded completely unconcerned. He could have been talking about going to the arcade or grabbing a cheeseburger.

"I want to see Dylan." Mel pressed against Darro's arm, but it wasn't budging.

"Dylan, someone wants to see you," the girl called out and her voice pierced the quiet that had settled around the trees. There was no response for a moment or two and then they saw a small figure come out from another grouping of trees.

"Oh, thank God, Dylan. I'm glad you are alright. Everyone is so worried." Mel pushed underneath Darro's arm, scooting away from his grasp. She took a few steps toward Dylan but stopped short. His face looked weird, with a small, sly grin and a glint in his eye; it frightened her.

“I’m fine, Mel. I’ve never been better. Everything is fine.” Dylan’s voice sounded relaxed, not the voice of a kid who had just stolen a car and who would face serious problems from his father.

“You need to come with me now, we have to go find your dad. He’s on his way.” Mel held out her hand, but Dylan did not move.

“No, I don’t need to do that. I do what I like and right now, I want to stay here. With my friends. We have some trees to burn.” Dylan’s voice trailed off as the kids started to laugh. Hedy wondered where the other two kids were and what they were up to.

“Dylan, this is crazy. Stop acting like this. What has gotten into you?” Mel was practically crying, and the girl started laughing, mimicking her voice. Ana gave a loud hissing sound and the girl fell silent.

“Nothing has gotten into us, Mel. We realized we don’t have to listen; we can do what we want, when we want. Ever since the cave, we figured it out. Nothing matters.” Dylan walked away from the tree and joined his friends, who were nodding in unison behind him. In the distance behind them, Hedy could see the silhouette of a bonfire. The missing kids must have just started it.

The three of them were gone, slipping into the trees before anyone saw them go. The crows must have taken that as their sign because in a flurry of wings and cawing, they filled the air and headed in the direction of the bonfire.

“Dylan!” Mel yelled after him but with all the

noise from the crows, he likely couldn't hear her.

"We know where they are headed. Let's cross out of these trees into open space and come toward the bonfire from the other side. I don't relish an ambush in these close quarters." Darro led the way out of the thicket of cut Christmas trees and into the open space of the field, taking a right turn toward the bonfire. In the light of the flame, Hedy could see two new figures crossing the field toward them. One was almost carrying the other.

"Who is that?" Darro stepped in front of the group, protectively.

"I think it is Yami with Raluca." Hedy crossed from behind Darro and took a few steps toward the pair. Even in the dim light, she could tell it was them. *But was it some kind of trap?*

"Be careful, lass. We don't know what we are dealing with." Darro kept a grip on his bat as the group made their way toward the slow-moving pair. The kids were still nowhere to be seen.

"Yami, what has happened?" Hedy called out toward the figure and they paused until the group met up with them. In the flickering bonfire light, Hedy could plainly see that Raluca was in terrible shape.

"We have to get her some help. I will explain everything later. She is dying." Yami spoke plainly, her words flat and emotionless. Hedy felt a flash of anger, knowing that Raluca had been tortured and likely at Yami's hand.

"Is Lyssa involved?" Hedy reached out an arm

to help hold up the old woman but Darro beat her to it. With a swift motion, he scooped her up as if she weighed nothing more than a small sack of wet leaves.

"There isn't time for this. Lyssa is involved, yes, and we need to get out of here. She's called these crows and who knows what else to come help her." Yami started walking toward the car lot, but Hedy grabbed her arm and pulled her back.

"Hold on. There are kids here and we need to help them. We can't leave them to face whatever Lyssa is planning."

"You think those kids are at risk? They have been part of all this. Lyssa has been commanding them. They are her minions now." Yami's voice still sounded flat and unemotional, and Hedy found it just too much to bear.

"Explain yourself! What do you mean? You tortured Raluca - I felt you do it. Now you are helping her? You better tell us what is going on." Hedy heard her voice pierce the air between them, sharp as her elfish knife back home. She could remember exactly how much each moment in that cave felt for the old woman. The thought made her nauseous.

"The cave. It held a crystal, a crystal with dark power that was helping Lyssa to heal. It is the only thing that's keeping her alive. Those kids stumbled into the cave and became infected with it. Now its darkness eats them and they are doing her bidding. You are wasting time, time that the moroica doesn't have. We have to get her to safety. Lyssa had me torture her for information on the waystation network. She wants to destroy it." Yami sounded emotional for the first time and Hedy wondered what had happened in that cave to change her from torturer to rescuer.

"Hedy, you take the old woman back in your car. I'll stay and round up the kids; I can bring them back in my car. If they won't come, I can't force 'em, but maybe Dylan will come with Mel, at least. I don't wanna stick around here to see what happens next." Darro was cradling Raluca as if she were a fragile bird, fallen out of a nest. She was moaning softly in his arms.

Behind them, Hedy heard the sounds of voices beginning to chatter, mimicking the sound of crows. They turned to see all the kids in a ring facing the fire, screaming into the night, tossing boughs and chunks of trees into the blaze. Near them was a shadowy figure.

"Dylan, come away from there!" Mel shouted and ran toward the bonfire. As she ran toward them, crows began to swoop and dive toward her, trying to peck her face and her hands as she shielded her eyes. She thrashed wildly with the crowbar, trying to wave them off but they kept coming toward her.

"Mel!" Ana screamed and ran toward her; the crows began their aerial assault on her, and she too used her piece of wood as a shield and a weapon.

"Stay back, with me." Hedy heard Raluca whisper the words and she hollered for the girls to stop.

“Come back. Raluca says to come back!” Hedy screamed as loud as she could, hoping they could hear her over the sound of the dive-bombing crows. The girls turned and ran back, hunched over as far as they could to shield their faces. The crows stopped the attack.

“They are guarding her. Guarding the children.” Raluca’s voice scraped out the sounds of words. “I can help. But I must be closer. The crows must…” Raluca paused, catching her breath again.

“How can we get closer with those crows?” Hedy grabbed a tissue out of her pocket and handed it to Mel so she could dab at the scratches along her arms.

“I can help with that.” Yami said, shrugging off her jacket. She slipped out of her clothing before anyone knew what was happening.

The transformation was sudden and alarming to watch. Hedy heard herself gasp as she saw Yami’s body shift into a large fox with fur bristling from her body and two large tails swirling around her.

“What the bloody hell…” Darro muttered and Hedy didn’t know whether she should be frightened or amazed by the sight.

The huge fox turned away from them and then gave a loud high-pitched screaming howl, nothing like the wolf sound or dog growl that Hedy would have expected. It was a terrifying scream and the sound filled the air around them. Three more loud screams pierced the night. The crows, unsettled by the sound, were shifting and cawing but not budging from their ring around the fire. The kids themselves had gone quiet, watching with intent eyes.

From the edge of darkness at the far end of the field, Hedy saw them. Eyes gleaming from the bonfire, small reddish fur glinting in the light. First a pair, then three more, then two more came from the darkness, answering that monstrous call. Near the huge fox that had been Yami, a ring of foxes perched, waiting.

With some silent signal, the foxes turned and began their assault on the crows. They slunk along the ground, keeping their muzzles clear of any talons or beaks. With precision striking, their sharp needle teeth pierced the necks of any crow within their reach. The gurgling caws and the gnashing of the fox teeth filled Hedy's ears and turned her stomach, the whole thing horrifying.

"Mother Mary, saints preserve us," Darro muttered and the group watched the carnage as the foxes ripped the crows to pieces in front of them. Hundreds of crows took to the sky, shrieking as they flew into the darkness. The bonfire was surrounded by the corpses of savaged crows.

"Oh, my God," Hedy heard Mel breathe next to her. The large fox turned back toward the group and loped over toward them. The summoned foxes were drifting back into the night. With only moments between, the fox became a human again, crouching low toward the ground.

"We better hurry. The crows may not stay gone for long," Ana urged. She was the only one with the composure to say anything after what they witnessed. Yami dressed quickly beside them.

"Closer," Raluca said to Darro and he carried her closer to the bonfire. He had no idea what the old woman would do once he brought her there; she hardly seemed to have the energy to even rest in his arms.

"The stone. Get the stone." The voice rasped again and this time, Yami pulled a large orange crystal from the small cloth satchel at her side. It had a dull orange glow compared to the roar of the bonfire.

"Energy. We need energy to reverse the evil." Raluca shifted slightly, as if she were trying to get down from Darro's arms. The kids around the bonfire were beginning to move, restless at the sight of the stone. Lyssa's shadowy figure pulled closer to them. Hedy gasped to see her again. Now she was a dark and withered wraith instead of the red-haired nemesis that Hedy remembered so vividly.

"Give us the stone. If you don't, we'll jump into the fire," Dylan's voice called out to them, taking a step toward the bonfire. He was only a few feet from its flames.

"No!" Mel yelled at him, and she stepped toward him before Ana grabbed her arm.

"Don't, Mel. It might make him panic."

"We will jump into the fire if you don't give us

the stone. We want the stone," Dylan's voice called out again as the shadow was draped around him like a shroud.

"Quickly. Girl, hold the stone with me." Raluca pointed at Mel, pulling herself forward, and Darro set her lightly on the ground. Yami took the stone and placed it into Raluca's wrinkled hand. Mel took a step toward her and placed her own hand on top of the crystal. It was warm under her palm.

"Focus on the boy. Focus your love," the old woman rasped and Mel closed her eyes, thinking of Dylan. Love for the chubby baby, as a toddler who loved eating Cheerios, as a small boy who collected Matchbox cars, the nights on the swing set when he begged her to push him higher, the drawing he made for her that was still on their refrigerator, his smile when they rode the Scrambler at the Fair. Love for the shy boy who hugged her goodbye, even at twelve years' old.

She let every memory flood over her, every smell and taste and sound that she could remember. Every camping trip with gooey s'mores, every Christmas morning with breakfast casserole at her uncle's house. Every memory was a brick in the wall of love that her mind built; a bulwark against the horror of him standing by the fire. The stone under her hand was getting hotter, as if her hand were on a warming burner, but she didn't really notice it. She kept her mind in the memories, focusing everything she had Dylan's face.

"No!" One of the kids screamed into the night

and then, one by one, they fell to the ground, writhing as if snakes were thrashing inside every limb. The shadow hovered over them, but they kicked and thrashed at it.

Mel saw something else in her mind, another figure. A young woman, who must have been Raluca, when she was just a girl. The figure was in some old city, flanked by two figures that seemed cloaked in darkness. But the girl had a light around her, as if she glowed from it. The girl paused and turned to look at Mel and she heard the words echo in her own ears.

"This is a good way to die. I am glad I can bring some good with my final breath. The stone will be destroyed. The children will be saved. And, so too the waystations, though they will feel my loss. But this is a good death. I am happy." The young Raluca gave her a smile and then she gone from Mel's mind.

The stone beneath her hand seared hot and then went cold. Mel opened her eyes to see Raluca crumpled to the ground. The bodies of the children were silent and still, and the shadow was gone.

# CHAPTER TWENTY-FIVE

Mel ran to Dylan, who had fallen dangerously close to the fire. With no crows to stop her, she sprinted and reached his side in moments. She pulled his limp body away from the heat and cradled his head in her lap, lightly petting his hair.

"Dylan...Dylan...wake up," she murmured, keeping her voice far calmer than the panic she felt inside. What if he never woke up? What if the destruction of the crystal had destroyed him with it? She couldn't think of that or she would start screaming.

She watched his chest rise and fall; at least he was breathing, but his body was still against her. The other children were lying where they had fallen, softly breathing in the cold night air.

Darro, Yami, and Hedy were circled around the crumpled form of Raluca, but Ana had joined Mel, kneeling down next to her. She put her arm around Mel's shoulder and gave her a squeeze, saying nothing. Nothing she could say in this moment would help. No one knew whether Dylan would wake up or not.

It seemed ages while the only sounds were the crackling of the bonfire and the soft breathing of the children. Mel continued to stroke his hair, cradling his head in her lap as if he were just sleeping. Tears were clinging to her lashes, ready to fall down her cheeks.

“Mel, look. Over there, at the girl.”

Mel looked at the figure next to them and she saw the girl’s arm twitch slightly. Ana stood up and moved closer to the girl, crouching again when she reached her side.

“She’s waking up, Mel.” Ana heard a sharp intake of breath from Mel. If the girl was waking, then maybe Dylan would as well.

There were the slightest movements coming from the children and she watched Dylan’s still face for any flicker or twitch. After several still moments, she saw his eyelids flicker.

“Oh, thank God. He’s waking up, Ana.” Mel grabbed one of Dylan’s hands and gave it a squeeze. It was still warm from the bonfire.

“What happened?” The girl was the first to speak, with no trace of the mocking tone she had used earlier. Ana was helping her to sit up slowly.

“Take it easy. You are safe. Everything is alright.” Ana’s words were soothing and washed over the girl quietly. The other boys were beginning to sit up, blinking at the bright firelight in obvious confusion.

"Do you remember anything?" Mel spoke to the girl, but she kept her eyes fixed on Dylan's micro-movements.

"I remember going into a cave with a weird orange light. Then it seemed like I was dreaming. Like I was watching a dream version of me doing things, but I wasn't the one doing them. If that makes any sense. Are we at the tree farm? Where's my mom?" The girl was starting to look worried.

"We'll get you to your mom, don't worry. For now, you need to take it easy." Ana stood up and gave a signal toward Hedy, who broke away from the group and walked toward the fire.

"Mel?" Dylan's voice was quiet as he looked up at his cousin. One of her tears splashed down on his cheek and she quickly wiped it away.

"Hey, kiddo. You gave me a fright. But you are okay now. Everything is okay." She gave his hand another squeeze and before he could protest, she leaned down and kissed him on the head.

"Hedy, we need to get these kids to their parents. You better take Raluca back to your house before people start showing up. Mel and I can finish up here," Ana said, standing close to Mel again.

"Yes, if you think you two are alright, I think we should go. We can take Raluca back with us in Darro's truck. Can one of you drive the Corvair back later?" Hedy watched Ana look expectantly at Mel since Ana had no idea how to drive a car.

"Yes, I can drive it. We'll come back to the house after I call my uncle and all the kids get picked up. No idea how we'll explain all this, but we'll figure something out." Mel was already pulling her phone out of her pocket and pulling up her uncle's phone number.

"OK, see you soon." Hedy gave Ana and Mel a quick hug before turning to hurry back toward the retreating figure of Darro carrying the limp Moroica toward his truck.

* * *

Darro placed Raluca on the bed in her room. At the moment, they didn't know what to do with her, but it seemed the best place for her body. Hedy heard the stairs creaking as he came back downstairs to join the two women in the shop. They were sitting at a table, drinking tea.

"Well, now what?" Darro pulled out a wooden chair and lightly set his girth down.

Hedy took a deep breath, letting it all push past her lips before speaking.

"I will call the Concierge and inform them. They'll need to tell me what we do next. I can't imagine the death of their leader is going to be welcome news." Hedy raised the teacup to her lips and let the scent of chamomile drift around her before taking a sip. She needed to be calm. Would her waystation recover from this?

"And, no offense, but what about her?" Darro gestured toward the still figure of Yami seated to his right.

Hedy paused for a moment, looking at the Kitsune who watched her intently.Yami said nothing. "I'm not the police, Darro. I'll tell the Concierge what has happened, and after that, it is out of my hands." Hedy took another sip of tea.

"I'll make amends in my own fashion, whether the Concierge calls for it or not." Yami finally spoke, then raised her own cup and took a small sip.

"So that's it, then? The old woman dies, and you will 'make amends'?" Darro continued staring at Yami but she said nothing further.

"Darro, I suspect the Concierge will handle this situation fully. There is nothing we can do tonight, other than call them. And remember, she helped us save the children. We never would have saved them without her."

"What about Lyssa? Is she gone for good, finally?" Darro spoke the words but Hedy wondered the same thing.

"With the crystal destroyed, I don't know if she will ever regain her full power, but I wouldn't count on her being gone for good. You should all take care. She was going to use the Moroica to destroy the Concierge. She may still have that plan. And I will have to live with giving her the idea for it," Yami said with a measure of sadness in her voice. She would have to atone for the part she played in the old woman's death.

Hedy watched Darro's face soften a bit and he said nothing else. She poured him a cup of tea and passed the plate of scones to him.

"Try a scone, Darro. I believe you will be pleasantly surprised. Adelaide shared a secret she learned from your Granny Raith," Hedy told him, watching Darro pause in mid-bite of the crumbling scone. "It seems spirits can speak with one another. She asked your Granny for the recipe." Hedy smiled even though Darro's face had gone quite pale. Nevermind how long it had taken to get the information out of Adelaide; it was worth the effort. Living with Adelaide had made her forget that not everyone was used to ghostly communications from long dead grannies.

Before Darro could respond, there was a rap on the door. Hedy knew it wasn't Mel or Ana - they would have come right in. The closed sign was up so it wasn't likely a customer. She left the table and headed into the entry, which was still awash in silver light from the Christmas tree.

Hedy opened the door to find Michael standing on her porch. She must have looked shocked because he began to blush.

"I'm sorry for intruding, I just wanted to come by to see how you were after the incident at the market. If this is a bad time…" Michael took a step back from the door though Hedy was shaking her head.

"No, it's not a bad time. Well, it's not a good time, but what I mean is...oh, please come in." She opened the door for him, and he stepped into the entry. She really should have told him to come back another time, but for a moment, seeing him reminded her of better things. Things that did not involve a dead Moroica in her guest bedroom.

"Please, join us in the shop. We were just having some tea." Hedy led the way back to the table with Yami and Darro.

"Michael, this is my gardener, Darro, and a recent guest here, Yami. We've had a rather trying evening, so our apologies for not being in better spirits." Hedy pulled a chair out for Michael, who sat down at the table.

"I don't want to intrude. I was just worried after the brouhaha at the market that perhaps you might need a hand. Those children seemed to have wrecked the whole event. They stole a car not long after they tore down your display. Did you know that?" Michael said and Hedy gave him a small smile in return.

"Yes, we know about the car. The good news is that the children have been found and I think things will be getting back to normal for them." Hedy poured him a cup of tea but said nothing else to explain.

"Hedy, you do know that your friend is not human, yes?" Yami spoke for the first time in a while, looking squarely across the table at Michael.

"What are you on about?" Darro spoke before either Hedy or Michael could say anything.

"I know another shapeshifter when I see one, Darro. He's an imp," Yami said simply as if it were the most obvious thing in the world.

Michael began to rise from the table, but Hedy held out a hand on his forearm to stop him.

"Yes, I know. A friend told me, though I didn't know about the imp part. Michael, I'm sorry for this. I'm sure this isn't how you would have wished to start this conversation." Hedy could have imagined a dozen better ways to broach the subject with Michael, but maybe Yami's direct approach was for the best. No more secrets.

"Hedy, I really don't know what to say. I've never had this happen before. But…yes, I am an imp, if that makes a difference." Michael looked supremely uncomfortable as he spoke.

"'If that makes a difference'? How could it not? You're a bloody demon?" Darro stood up from the table. Shapeshifting foxes, possessed children, and now a demon sitting at table - it was too much for him. He needed to get home and get pissed drunk.

"Darro!" Hedy tried to say more but Michael interrupted her.

"No, Hedy, it's fine. Really. Now you know why I don't lead with that piece of information. Yes, I am a demon, Darro. Well, not really, not in the way you think. An imp is not a full demon with the power to possess others or take souls. I haven't done the…things…that are required for that full transformation. As an imp, I have only minor powers and abilities. Even those, I try not to use. I am trying to lead a normal life." Michael finished speaking, quite sure he hadn't begun to answer their questions.

"Well, I am going home. I need a drink and a smoke and to be away from this craziness for the night. I'll be back next week, Hedy. Call if you need me before then." Darro gave a nod to Hedy before heading toward the entry.

The door creaked open and Darro gave a roaring "Hallo," causing Hedy to jump up from the table.

A familiar voice said, "Hedy, do you have room for a salamander who has come back?" Around Darro's large frame, she saw Bren Aldebrand standing there, suitcase in hand. All the words she had wanted to say to him for the last few weeks flew right out of her mind.

# SWEET TOOTH AND CLAW

## *A Gingerbread Hag Mystery - Book Three*

Available Now!

Be sure to sign up for the newsletter at www.kamiltimore.com for more information on upcoming books and giveaways. If you liked this book, please leave a review on Amazon and Goodreads and help spread the word. Join my Facebook Author Page @kamiltimore

# *Biography*

K. A. Miltimore is a writer living in the Pacific Northwest who has followed the advice of her 5th grade teacher, Miss Hammond, and become a writer. She loves mid-century fashion, 80s music and nachos (not necessarily in that order). With her husband and son, she loves exploring quirky local towns, and dreams of dragging them both to Iceland for a tour someday. Her tombstone will likely read "Always Creating". In addition to writing, she enjoys making jewel spiders, looking for great Washington red wines, and re-watching the movies that she has forgotten over the years.

CPSIA information can be obtained
at www.ICGtesting.com
Printed in the USA
FSHW021953020220
66761FS